The Measure of the Universe

Ellen Larson

He gave men speech, and speech created thought,
Which is the Measure of the Universe.

Prometheus Unbound, II 50–51
Percy Bysshe Shelley

Saga SF

2002

The Measure of the Universe

Cover by Robert A. Gutowski

Published by
Saga SF
473 17th St. #6
Brooklyn, NY 11215-6226

http://savvypress.com/sagasf/index.html
Email sagasf@savvypress.com
Fax: 1-443-238-0770

Printed in the United States of America

ISBN 0-9669877-4-8
LCCN 2001099448

The Measure of the Universe

Through the bubble window of the aircraft, R.H. Herman gazed down at the sapphire blue Mediterranean, and at the rugged little gray-green islands dotting its surface. The expanse of the sea and the sparseness of the land made him feel a little queasy. He was a long way from home, and an even longer way out on a spindly professional limb of his own grafting. Unnerving to think that what happened in this stagnant little backwater of civilization might determine the future of the entire planet—not to mention his whole career! A trickle of sweat, inspired by the blazing Mediterranean sun, ran down the back of his neck. His wife had been right: he shouldn't have worn the suit.

The pilot singled out a conical island on the hazy strip where the water met the sky and pointed the aircraft at it. Before long Herman made out a white boardwalk ringing a placid harbor. Colorful sailing vessels were moored along long white piers that shot out into the water like the teeth of a semicircular comb. Behind the marina the ground rose steeply, so that the little houses, painted creamy white and blue and salmon pink, appeared stacked on top of one another like children's blocks. Above the houses, the land continued to rise to a stubby gray-green peak, upon which goats grazed, or dozed in the shade of stunted olive trees.

The craft soared over the southern tip of the marina, swooped behind the spur of the mountain, and floated noiselessly down to a bulls-eye landing pad. With an ease born of long practice, Herman

3

popped open the passenger door and hopped out into a thick wall of heat.

A marine, dressed in crisp whites, emerged from a little building and approached along a walkway marked off by red geraniums. His salute had an extra snap that filled Herman with confidence. The man was obviously aware, despite the lack of attendant fanfare, that he was in the presence of power—or at least, of potential power. After a minimal exchange, the marine pointed out the service tunnel that ran beneath the spur to the marina. Hefting his briefcase, Herman set out upon the last stage of his journey.

Ω   Ω   Ω

An hour later, Herman's progress ground to a halt half way up a steep stone stairway—the fourteenth he had climbed since leaving the marina. Breathing hard, he dropped the briefcase onto the step above and tried to straighten up. Stairs! An anachronism in a world that had discovered the graviton and its antiparticle half a century ago. Probably kept around for the tourists. Tourists took such pathetic delight in the inconveniences of the olden days.... Putting his hands on his hips, he arched his back. His wife was right: he needed to get to the gym more often. He grimaced at a hanging basket of pink and white flowers. It was becoming a real question how much more he could take.

"Don't worry, mister!"

Herman looked up.

The street urchin who had guided him through the maze of twisting lanes, keeping the peddlers and goats at bay, grinned at him from the top of the stairs. "That address you want is right here." The boy threw his fist over his shoulder, pointing with his thumb.

Taking heart, Herman retrieved his briefcase and pulled himself up the final climb. He followed the boy to the gate of a cream-colored cottage perched on a jutting lip of the mountain.

The front door was painted blue, as were the shutters and roof. A dense, leafy plant with yellow flowers like miniature trumpets climbed up the stucco walls and shaded the windows. Pots of geraniums squatted on either side of the door. A wrought-iron bench, its green paint beginning to chip, afforded a postcard view of the marina far below.

Quaint. It would make a nice weekend rental—except for that climb.

The urchin was shuffling his feet. Herman remembered himself and reached for his wallet. The boy took a moment to record payment and issue a receipt, then loped away like one of the goats, the red scarf that held his white blouse snug to his waist fluttering behind him.

There was no vox patch, not even a doorbell. Herman lifted a brass knocker and let it drop. It fell two centimeters and stuck. He pushed down on the gargoyle head until it hit home with a thud.

"It's open, Mr. Herman." The voice was deep for a woman's, which gave the hint of reproof a little extra muscle.

Herman turned the doorknob and stepped across the threshold into cave-like darkness.

"How much did he charge?" The voice came from somewhere to his right.

He turned toward the sound, removing his sunglasses. "Twenty credits." There she was, sitting at a sleek computer console at the back of the room.

"Tch." The disapproval was clear, now. "The going rate is seven. You should have let me handle it."

"Just doing my bit to prop up the local economy." As his eyes began to adjust, he looked around. To the left, a massive gray stone sat on a table in an otherwise unfurnished area. To the right, two chairs were snugged up on either side of a table set with drinks. "There doesn't seem to be much going on around Kimolos...."

"And in any event you'll write it off as a business expense and let the taxpayers foot the bill. Don't just stand there, Mr. Herman. Have a seat." She waved a hand at the table and chairs. "That's iced tea in the pitcher.... Of course you did not stop to consider that you only encourage those boys to gouge the tourists. They should be in school where they belong."

"It's July, Dr. Thanau." He laid his jacket over the back of a sofa cluttered with boxes and went to sit at the table.

"Then they should be out playing and having fun. Today's youth is obsessed with making money. Not that I expect you to find anything wrong with that...."

Herman flashed a smile as he gave his host the once over with eyes fully adjusted to the gloom: a spare-boned woman wearing a loose, scoop-necked dress—a galabeya, she had called it—with dark eyes above a wide mouth, her gray hair pulled upwards from forehead and neck. She had made no move to stop working, or to join him. He shifted his hip and pulled a handkerchief from his back pocket. "You haven't changed." He wiped at the sweat behind his ears. "A little thinner; a little grayer."

"A little more impatient." The keypads clicked beneath her long fingers.

So much for small talk about old times to break the ice…. "Then I'll skip the intro about professional opportunity and civic duty and get right to the point." He returned the hanky to his pocket and reached for the pitcher. "I need your help."

"Obvious—or you would never have left your overstuffed office with the view of the Lincoln Memorial to visit an ugly old woman who doesn't like you."

He tipped the pitcher and watched the amber liquid arc through the air, foaming a little as it hit the side of the glass. "A little crustier…." He spoke in awe rather than anger. "I didn't think it was possible."

The keypads clicked away.

Herman took a sip of tea. Hard as nails; no subtlety. No wonder she hadn't been able to cut it in the big leagues…. "As I wrote in my letter, the UN Commission on Negami-Earth Relations has received the first batch of research proposals from the Negami mission in Virginia. We've agreed to select a pilot project within the next two weeks. The Negami are thrilled. They've sent out five hundred invitations to a black-tie dinner to commemorate the event. Since we've been stalling them at every turn for five years—while they've been patient and jumped through all our hoops as fast as we could manufacture them—you might think their confidence is a little naive. But the truth is, we've run out of excuses. We either keep our end of the bargain or admit we never had any intention of letting them carry out their so-called non-invasive studies." And if that didn't pique her curiosity, nothing would…. "By the way. Where do you stand on the issue of Negami contact?" He took another sip of tea.

She raised her heavy eyebrows. "Me? What could it possibly matter what I think? Oh, very well…. I have no interest in them—other than the usual idle curiosity...how many eyes do they have, what do they eat, how do they reproduce. Well—I do get a tickle out of watching the religious right trying to corral the theological implications of a sentient species from another solar system. And, conversely, I am somewhat pained to realize that fifteen years of dealing with that species has not yet had the unifying effect on international politics anticipated by the globalists. But of course it was a crushing blow when the Negami set up their mission in the US...as if your President were the leader of Earth. Divisive, shortsighted...."

"The Security Council voted twenty three to nothing in favor of the location."

She waved his remark aside. "And I will also admit to a sincere hope that they are telling the truth when they say they want nothing more than to study our archaic Earth culture to satisfy their academic curiosity. But I don't fret about the unpleasant alternatives, if that's what you're asking. I'm a busy woman, and alien biology is not my field. Speaking of which, I hope you haven't come here on a wild goose chase, Mr. Herman...."

"I don't think so...."

"Because you were never known for your grip on the fundamental distinctions between one scientific discipline and another...."

"Ah, but the course I took from you was unforgettable, Doctor."

"It did at least fulfill what your benighted university system referred to as your 'science requirement.'"

"And allowed me the opportunity of meeting you."

She rolled her eyes. "Oh, please!"

Herman held up a hand. "I'm serious, Doctor. I'm still your biggest fan in Washington. Despite what happened."

Her lips tightened into a chilly smile. "Which does nothing to enlighten me as to why you, an advisor to a high-powered UN Commission, want to know what I, your former communication sciences professor, think about the Negami."

"I'm getting there. So I may take it you don't particularly resent them; you're not afraid of them?"

"I wouldn't waste my time."

"That's what I wanted to hear. Because if you were, you couldn't help me." He studied the water droplets that had beaded and run

7

down the outside of his glass. This was where it got tricky…. "Here's the problem. Truth is, CONER is splitting at the seams. The Commissioner doesn't buy it that our visitors have 'come in peace.' He thinks the policy of *entente cordiale* is facilitating a secret Negami plan to learn as much about Earth as possible in preparation for invasion. He sees even the most desiccated research proposal they submit as a clever assault on Earth's sovereignty. In lock step with the Pentagon, he hammers the President with demands for military preparedness and complete noncooperation. In fairness I have to point out that the Negami's refusal to share their knowledge, while at the same time begging us to share ours, only supports the Commissioner's position. The Secretary, on the other hand, continues to preach patience, and the dangers of bringing about a crisis of confidence. I don't mind admitting that she represents the opinion of a significant number of European and African governments. She sends a weekly memo to the President reminding him that in fifteen years the Negami haven't shown the slightest sign of aggression. In her opinion, we have an obligation to take them at their word until we have evidence that we shouldn't. The Commissioner says the Secretary is compromising the future of the planet with her pacifism. The Secretary says the Commissioner is provoking confrontation with his militarism. The President, of course, is in the middle, and wants to have it both ways so that whatever happens no one can say he was on the wrong side."

The click of keypads had ceased. "Should you be telling me this in such graphic terms, Mr. Herman?"

"You have clearance."

"Correction. I had clearance ten years ago, for about six minutes."

Herman wiped the water from the outside of his glass. "You've been reinstated."

"On whose authority? I have agreed to nothing. Obvious—as you have not yet told me what you want from me."

"On *my* authority. I knew I needed to explain the situation to get your cooperation, but I can't explain it unless you have clearance. So I, ah, pulled some strings."

"Don't you risk your reputation if I turn you down? I didn't hear you asking me to keep quiet about this. What if I blab to the press?"

He drained his glass and reached for the pitcher. "That's a risk I'm willing to take. You're too intelligent to go along with what I have in mind without knowing all the ramifications. Besides, I happen to know you're a woman of integrity." Even scientists have egos....

She thrust her square chin forward, moving her lower lip back and forth. Finally she stood and came out from behind the console. "Pour me a glass, will you, Mr. Herman?" She sat opposite him. "And continue ramifying."

He filled her glass and set it down in front of her. "Three months ago the Secretary appointed a confidential task force to come up with ideas for ending the stalemate. I'm on it. Chairperson."

"Congratulations. Your career continues to skyrocket."

"Maybe." So, she knew about his swift rise to power.... "I admit I feel like I'm at the crossroads of something big. My analysis of the situation and proposal were recommended by the task force, and then approved and adopted by the Commission. Yesterday, the Secretary asked me to implement my plan."

"Please try to be more specific, Mr. Herman."

He watched her raise the glass to her lips. "Now, where have I heard you say that before?"

"It must have been on your final exam, when you referred to Homer as 'an early European author who produced many famous works.'"

Herman chuckled. "I wish I had your memory!" And that was no mere flattery.... "Well, I may not have studied my Homer, but I've put in the hours over this one. Here's the key point: the Negami are far more technologically advanced than we are—they managed to cross some sixty-odd light-years of space to get here, right? Lucky for us, they are also highly civilized."

"A philosopher might suggest that luck had nothing to do with it."

He met her sarcasm with a smile. "People were scared at first, but the Negami have obeyed our laws and behaved themselves as if they had dropped in from Japan instead of somewhere in the constellation Taurus. Even the average joes are getting used to the idea that, as they used to say, 'we are not alone.' And the eggheads hold the collective opinion that there is no point in worrying about them at all—since they clearly have the ability to conquer us, or destroy us, or make us dance the cha-cha if they want to, and there's not a damned thing we can do about it."

"Having not been in a coma the last fifteen years, I'm familiar with this argument." She picked up her glass. "Did you say this was *your* analysis?"

He took it on the chin again. Sometimes you swallowed a few insults in a worthy cause.... "No. *This* is my analysis: they want to study us; they are dying to get their hands on our funny little old-fashioned culture. Well, what if we turn this on its head and use it to our own advantage? You're the one who taught me that learning is a duplex communication; that the teacher also learns from the student."

"Did I say that?"

"Yes. But don't worry, you weren't talking about me."

"I didn't think so." She pushed at the wisps of hair on her forehead.

"So I thought—what if we study them while they study us? What have we got to lose? I'll tell you what: nothing. Our potential gain must outweigh theirs by a staggering degree. In fact, it is statistically impossible for them to learn anything about us that will harm us, because, given a sum of Earth knowledge x, the difference between their knowledge gained plus x and our knowledge gained plus x must always have a negative value for them, and a positive value for us."

"Two steps forward and one back for us; two steps backward and one forward for them."

"Exactly. And the beauty of it is that all the Commissioner's worries are turned against him. He's afraid of the Negami because they are smarter and more powerful than us, so he thinks we're in danger from them. But actually there's only one way to change that, and that's to learn from them. And since we don't have the technology to go to their planet, we can't study them unless they stay here!"

She made a circular motion with her hand, like a stage manager telling the actors to move it along. "So by refusing their request to study us and trying to get them to leave Earth, we are throwing away our only opportunity to study them and lessen the technology gap. Yes, I'm with you Mr. Herman. I doubt that your analysis is as original as you think. What about your proposal?"

He folded his hands across his stomach. However much she downplayed her interest, he knew it was there—it had to be in someone with such a mind as hers.... "To let them conduct their research; let them study us—while we carry out a shadow program to study them. Nothing overt—oh no—but a systematic effort aimed at maximizing our opportunities to nibble their technology away from them, piece by minuscule piece, in a way they'll never notice."

He gave her time to react, but she said nothing, nor did her expression change. Sometimes it was like talking to stone.... "All parties have agreed to the basics," he continued. "Of course the Commissioner will only go along if he has approval over the choice of research proposals. Fortunately, the Negami understand that, for cultural reasons they don't necessarily understand, or in national security interests they may not be able to perceive clearly, we may reject some proposals. As far as the plan goes, it doesn't matter how obscure the research is. It's the background information we're after—everyday things the Negami take for granted, bits of knowledge they consider insignificant, but which may be the building blocks of knowledge for our scientists. Now, here's where it gets slick...."

He leaned his elbows on the table. No matter how many times he heard it, the cleverness of it thrilled him.... "The Negami insist that their researchers be anonymous, so that their data will be 'authentic.' In the Commissioner's eyes, this was the biggest sticking point. He wanted them to be surrounded by marines in full body armor. But what no one seemed to realize—until I brought it up—was that when they are 'in the field' doing their research, they will be vulnerable! They want to keep it low key? No escorts, total anonymity? Great! Whatever equipment they bring with them will be unguarded—at least occasionally. It won't be the really high-ticket items, but it'll be something, maybe something as innocuous as a Negami toothbrush, or a careless word let slip over dinner. And we'll be there to catch it!"

"Ingenious."

He sighed, and leaned back in his chair. "The Negami proposals stipulate that their researchers should be assigned to counterparts in the appropriate field. That's the norm in the scientific community, right?"

"I believe it is."

"We'll use this concept to get our people close to them, so that we can make the most of it when they let their guard down in a friendly environment. We don't care if the information seems insignificant, or if we don't understand it at first. We're in this for the long haul. It'll be like putting together a puzzle—the biggest puzzle Earth has ever seen—one piece at a time."

He kept his eyes on her face. "All we need are people from the international scientific and academic communities involved—key people who will coordinate with the Commission, and with my task force." He crossed his legs and settled back in his chair. "It's a simple plan, really. But it satisfies both the Secretary's mandate of *entente* and the Commissioner's mania for taking action towards self-preservation."

At that she stirred. "And your President's desire to stay on the fence. Mr. Herman, I see where you are headed, and I don't know whether to laugh or...laugh. If my memory, which you admire so much, has neither thinned nor gone gray, you can have no possible expectation that I would agree to work for your government—or, for that matter, that your government would ever let me darken its rotunda again."

"It's not my government. It's the UN. You've been pre-approved, on the Secretary General's authority. No questions asked."

"Mr. Herman! Why on Earth would you go to this extent?"

"Because, damn it, the future of the planet is at stake and this is no time for amateurs! Because Aisha Thanau is the best."

A breeze rippled down the mountain side and made the green curtain of leaves over the windows sway. Her dark eyes glittered beneath half-closed lids. "I am an academician, Mr. Herman, not a secret agent."

"Look. I've staked my whole future on the success of this plan. Do you think I haven't thought it through?" He allowed his anger to show, just a touch.... "You are a Nobel Prize winner and a renowned expert in communications technology. In your day, you have been a consultant to a dozen world leaders. You are tough as nails and smart as a whip."

"Do you mean that for flattery or insult?"

"It's just a fact." He was confident now. He had hooked her, he could hear it in her voice: she was mouthing the characteristic sarcasm, but the sting was gone. "You'll take it in stride where others would panic. No one will ever suspect anything is going on. In fact, nothing will be going on—you'll just be doing what you do. You'll probably end up writing the seminal book on Negami linguistics."

"And you promised not to bait me with visions of professional advancement."

"You can take the opportunity or leave it." He made it sound like it was nothing to him. "I know I'd take it. But there's more at stake than that: what you'll be doing for humanity. What we learn from you and, hopefully, from others that will follow, could benefit a hundred different scientific fields. Astronomy! Physics! Bioengineering! Medicine! Think what we can learn from the Negami, if we are only clever enough to find a way past their defenses! We might make a century's advance in five minutes with the right information."

He raised his glass to his lips, but did not drink. Instead, he watched her face—he saw her lips twitch, and a far-away look come to her eyes.

"You are the perfect choice for the pilot project." His tone was matter-of-fact, dismissive of doubt. "You have resources even the Negami will not expect."

"You think so." She smirked at him. "I admit when you first contacted me, I thought you had some idea of using my devices to eavesdrop on the Negami mission."

"Nothing so overt—but no doubt your technologies will come in handy."

"I see. Mr. Herman, despite your grandiose presentation, it sounds to me that your plan is simply to lull these superintelligent aliens into overconfidence by confronting them with an eccentric professor who is known to have been shunned by the establishment."

"Yes."

She nodded, pulling her mouth into a deep frown, the lower lip jutting out again. Then she gave a snort. "Just what are you asking me to do—specifically?"

He opened his briefcase and pulled out a blue folder. "We've got a request to conduct research on early forms of communication. That's right up your alley." He opened the folder and put his finger on the first page. "Paleography. That's the study of early writing, right?"

"My years spent teaching were not wholly in vain."

He gave a good-humored chuckle, as one conspirator to another. "It's a low-priority proposal—last on their list of fifty. Researcher's name is Titek. The topics he mentions are dry as dust." He flipped through the folder. "No offense. The point is this one is so harmless it doesn't threaten the Commissioner. Uh…." He turned a page. "He mentions an interest in epigraphy—what's that?"

"The study of inscriptions on rocks and tablets."

"Right. Then he goes on about phonemics. I guess it's a typo and he means phonetics."

"No, he's correct. A phoneme is any one of a set of distinctive speech elements or sounds in a language. All languages have a different set of phonemes—that's where little accents come from. Did you come for a lesson in philology?"

Herman closed the folder and placed a hand on its plastic cover. "No. I came because I want you to be Titek's counterpart." He looked up at her and smiled. "I think you've just proved you're an ideal match. You can fill him in on everything he wants to know about potsherds and dead sea scrolls—he'd probably love to hear about Homer. It'll all be above board—except we'll debrief you periodically, and set up some unobtrusive surveillance as opportunities present themselves. He'll never know anything is going on. That's the beauty of having a real scientist such as yourself involved."

"I hope you're not underestimating this gentleman."

"I don't think so…. I've met him. Very scholarly, rather delicate in appearance…not exactly an Adonis. He's had the same superficial surgery they all have, by the way, so he looks all right."

"Why would I possibly care what he looks like?"

"I just mean, he'll pass as human. We don't want the neighbors swarming around ogling the alien. No hoopla. Just another visiting research scientist. I probably shouldn't admit this…but I've told him all about you, and he's dying to meet you. So what do you say?"

He watched her face, trying to gauge her reaction. Had she bought the story? Selling it had been like walking a tightrope between triumph and disaster. But he knew her so well: the love of knowledge;

the attraction to power; the egocentricity that blinded her to failure.

She raised the glass of iced tea and sipped delicately. "It's a tempting offer, although it will throw my schedule on the new book all to hell. But...I think we might be able to come to an agreement. In the interests of science."

A tight-lipped smile spread slowly across his face, and his eyes shone with a cold triumph he did not bother to hide.

Ω   Ω   Ω

As always, Aisha sat at her console, lost in her work, a comm loop fitted to her ear. Her long fingers tapped relentlessly at the keypads, or manipulated the virtual hand—the invention of which had changed the face of computers forty years before by eliminating the need for the old-fashioned cursor. Using the Plex, she sifted the archives of human knowledge for patterns of facts in the fields of interest to her. Sometimes—quite often if she maintained the proper environment—the patterns coalesced into ideas. Then, roaming free and unfettered in her mind, she would nurture those ideas with her thoughts until they blossomed into words. And when the words were full-blown, she would preserve them at the peak of their power and beauty on the pages of her books. It was a magical process—random and unpredictable, but inevitable, too, like the breakdown of an unstable isotope. It was also her life, her joy, and wholly consuming. No matter that the sun had set; no matter that she had forgotten to make or eat her lunch; no matter that she was expecting a house guest from so many light-years away—

Her fingers ceased their tapping. Well.... That one did rather take her breath away. She had not admitted as much to Herman three weeks before, but the chance to meet a being from another planet...who wouldn't be excited by it? Except those religious absolutists, of course.... And that he should be a paleographer! What a professional plum to have fall out of the blue into her lap! To be the very first.... Not that Herman could possibly understand what such an opportunity meant to a real scholar—he only cared about power; prestige; money.

What she needed was a good stretch. She got up and opened the door. Perhaps she would be able to hear her visitor coming....

The jasmine-scented breeze rolling up the steep mountain side carried the faint sounds of music from the cafés in the marina. Children were playing football a few streets away—the sounds of shoe hitting ball alternated with their shouts. The neighbor's cat rubbed against her legs and levitated onto the window sill beneath her hand. She stroked the cat obligingly, then reached her arms to the sky and rotated her shoulders in a circle for a few minutes. For a few minutes longer, she listened for the sounds of footsteps on the stairway, then went back inside. As an afterthought, she turned on the lights.

Ω   Ω   Ω

Titek stood before the blue door and put a thoughtful forefinger to his lips. Insects with large white wings flitted about a yellow globe that hung from a bracket above the mailbox. A large yellow cat stared at him from the nearby window sill. The gargoyle on the door stuck its tongue out at him. Taking a deep breath, he hopped up onto the stone stoop, crouching low to keep out of the flight pattern of the insects.

"Dr. Thanau?"

Inside, Aisha's fingers paused over the keypads. "It's open." She slipped the comm loop from her ear and listened.

Still bending low, Titek opened the door a crack. "I am Titek, Dr. Thanau. I am here."

"I believe you." She stood and stepped around the console. "Please come in."

"Nothing would give me greater pleasure, but I hesitate to open the door further for fear that the gargantuan insects gathered about your lamp will seize the opportunity with which fortune has presented them and enter with me."

"They're just moths," said Aisha. "They won't do any harm." She reached the door and opened it wide. "Welcome to Kimolos."

Titek straightened up, compressing his lips into a V-shaped smile. "Thank you," he said, and stepped inside. "I'm very pleased to meet you." He gave the hand she held out a limp-fingered shake. "You are very kind to offer sanctuary to a stranger from so far, far away."

"Not really." She closed the door and gestured toward the sofa (cleared of the boxes). "I have hosted many visiting colleagues in my

16

day, and have myself been hosted. It is quite common in scientific circles."

Titek bowed. "This is a noble tradition that has found its way between the stars, for it is one and the same on my world. By treating me as a visiting colleague, you make me feel more welcome than I could have wildly dreamed possible." He bent his knees and sank down into the soft cushions of the sofa.

Aisha opened her mouth, closed it, and sat in a chair opposite. "I read through your scope of work. I think I'll be able to help you answer many of your questions regarding early writing systems. Time frames, implements, and so on."

"I look forward to hitting the books under your tutelage!" he said eagerly. "I am very lucky to have the chance to meet the preeminent scholar in the field. I only hope I do not make of myself...a pain in the neck. Is that the correct phrase?"

"Yes. And I must say I'm impressed. Your English is extraordinary. Your people must have a natural faculty for languages."

"Ah, thank you!" His smile widened, revealing small white teeth. "I have studied extensively since the first moment I was able to get my mitts on your language database. But I must fess up and admit that yes, we do have a certain pre-existing...faculty...."

"How many Earth languages have you studied?"

His eyes widened. "There is more than one?"

Aisha chuckled. "Living languages? About three hundred."

"Goodness gracious me!"

"And that's not counting dialects."

"Gadzooks!" He jockeyed forward through the cushions to the edge of the sofa. "I have only heard about English! Our mission scouts reported that all Earthers spoke English! Of course," he said, as if trying to be fair, "they are not specialists in the field of languages, and it might not have occurred to them to poke around for more."

"We do all speak English. But only for the last half century or so, since universal communication stabilized."

"So recently...."

"Some countries tried to hold out...the French...r

sal, of course, I mean...."

He waved a hand. "Of course...."

"But the regional languages continue to thrive and are generally coequal with English. You'll hear people speaking Greek here on Kimolos. That is the national language of Greece."

"Greek." Titek blinked. "'It's Greek to me.' Ah!" He looked at Aisha in astonishment. "Now I understand!"

"Congratulations." Aisha cleared her throat. "But I'm forgetting my duties. It's a long trip from Virginia. You must be hungry?"

"You are very gracious. I could eat a horse—metaphorically speaking, of course. I trust they told you I am a stickler for vegetarianism?"

"Certainly. Why don't I show you to your room, and you can unpack while I fix supper. I'll warm up—"

"Unpack." Titek smacked a hand to his head and sprang to his feet. "I have left my outcases suitside!" He turned and bolted to the door.

"Don't worry...," began Aisha.

Titek wrenched open the door. The cat sprang from atop one of the suitcases and disappeared into the night. Dodging the moths, Titek pulled his belongings inside. "Thank goodness they are safe!" He leaned against the closed door and put a hand over his heart. "The whole of my personal possessions as well as several important instruments are locked safe and sound inside. I am knocked down by a feather to find that I could be so careless as to forget them."

"They would have been safe." Aisha stood. "Don't let it upset you."

"But it is not like me!" His hand fluttered to his head, and smoothed back his bits of hair. "Perhaps I have lost my marbles in the excitement of finally achieving my greatest desire."

"That must be it. Have you been...working toward this achievement for a long time?"

"Fourteen years."

"Well then! I'd better break out the champagne. That is, if you can...?"

"Oh yes. As long as I do not overindulge."

"Wise words in any language. Then we'll celebrate your success later on. I remember the night my first grant was approved.... Well. Let me show you to your room." She headed for the narrow staircase ¹ ⁄ided the front of the house in two.

Titek looked at the suitcases. "I think it advisable if I make two trips. They weigh a ton, and I have already raised a blister on my thumb."

Aisha turned on the landing and frowned at him. "Didn't the boy carry them for you?"

"One of them. But he was so pint-sized, and the way so very steep. I could not bear to watch him carry them both."

"How much did he charge you?"

"Ten credits. Was that too much?"

"The going rate is seven."

"Yes, but it was after dark, and there was the suitcase."

"True," said Aisha, and she turned and continued up the stairs.

Titek left one suitcase at the foot of the stairs and hauled the other up. At the top he found himself in a narrow hallway, with two doors on either side. The nearest on the right was open, so he headed for that, clutching the suitcase in front of him with two hands.

He found Aisha standing in the middle of a small, lemon-yellow room with a slanting white ceiling. Against one wall there was a low bed made of red wood, covered with a blue quilt. A wardrobe, made of the same wood, stood opposite. A long, narrow window, set low beneath the eaves, looked down upon the marina.

Dropping the suitcase with a thud, Titek went to the window and stooped, placing his hands on his knees. "Goodness gracious me!"

"Will this do?" asked Aisha. "It's a bit plain, I imagine, for someone as, uh, well-traveled as yourself."

"Do? Oh, my, yes. It is...majestic." He straightened up, careful not to bump his head, and turned around. The inner wall was decorated with half a dozen prints in blue frames. "Oh! These are wonderful!" He approached the one by the door. "What is the place these paintings depict with such exactitude?"

"Nineteenth Century Egypt. They are reproductions of the David Roberts' watercolors."

"Astounding! Where is Egypt?"

"On the southern side of the Mediterranean Sea. My father was Egyptian, so I have a special affection for the place."

"Oh!" He put his hands behind his back. "Such breadth, such colors.... And this one! The way the cluster of stone pillars rises out of the desolate sand! I am falling all over myself wondering what these symbols mean!"

Aisha raised her eyebrows. "That's the Temple of Sobek at Kom Ombo. And I'm impressed you recognized the hieroglyphs as more than mere design."

"Oh? But the repetitive patterns cry out for interpretation, do they not?"

"I believe they do. Perhaps later we can answer their call. But right now I'm going to start supper. Your bathroom is just across the hall. Come down whenever you like. Half an hour."

When she had left, Titek went to the center of the room and stood with clasped hands. There was a white vase, empty, on top of the dresser. There was a little table lamp with a pink seashell shade on the bedside table. There—

He heard the crash, and the groan that followed it, and fled the room with a gasp.

From the landing, he saw Aisha sprawled out on the floor next to the suitcase, her thin legs akimbo. He pattered down the steps and fell to his knees by her side.

"Eeaa! Are you hurt?"

She sat up slowly and put her hand to her head, where she found the comm loop dangling from her hair. "I don't think so. Damned thing." She disentangled the plastic earpiece and put it in her pocket. "Next time I'm going for the implant."

"What...what...eeaa!" His voice shook, but he spoke slowly and softly. "I don't understand what's happening. Eeaa! You are injured. Tell me what to do."

Aisha reached out and found the back of the sofa. "You don't have to do a thing, thank you. I'm fine." She pulled herself up and straightened her galabeya.

Titek followed her as she headed to the back hallway. "This is not true! There is something wrong. You...you fell over the suitcase. Did you not see it?"

Aisha entered the bathroom and turned on the tap. "No, I didn't." She ran water over a washcloth, wrung out the excess, and held it to her forehead.

Titek stood in the doorway. "I don't understand."

She ran the washcloth around the back of her neck. "They didn't tell you." It was a statement, not a question. "Typical."

"Didn't tell me what?"

She dropped the washcloth into the sink and came to the door. "I'm blind. Do you know that word?"

"Yes."

"Good. Now, if you don't mind. Unless you're blind, too." She slammed the door in his face.

Ω   Ω   Ω

Titek, planted amidst the cushions on the sofa, raised his head when he heard the bathroom door open. He placed his folded hands in his lap and waited. But Aisha did not reappear. A minute later, he heard the sound of cupboards being opened and closed.

He arose from the sofa and tiptoed down the back hallway again. Peeking through an open door, he saw her standing by a counter, shredding lettuce into a bowl.

He held out his clasped hands. "Dr. Thanau. I am much distressed. May I ask you please to take a moment of your valuable time and explain to me how it can be that you are blind—in this day and age of enlightenment?"

Aisha moved the bowl aside and picked up a knife and a large tomato. "I fail to see that it matters."

"Oh, but it does!" Titek unclasped his hands and held them in front of him, palms up. "We understood that your scientific knowledge was well above the level where such things were still possible. Physical infirmity is unknown to us. Physical well-being…freedom from disease…these are considered the bare essentials of civilization. It is against our way, our law, as you would call it, to intrude upon a society that has not yet reached a certain minimum standard. Our scouts reported that your society was very sophisticated in medical matters. Why have you not had a transplant, or robotic implant? Please."

Aisha pursed her lips as she sliced. "Your scouts seem to have missed a few details. Tch. I suppose I'd better give you a little history lessen." She waved the knife towards the breakfast table. "Sit."

Titek pulled a stool out from under the table and sat. "I am all an

21

ear."

"Then I trust I won't have to repeat myself." She went to the refrigerator and pulled out a loaf of bread. "When I was fourteen I fell into an irrigation ditch in Syria. Later I developed an eye infection, bacterial, presumably from the water. The doctors couldn't clear it up; couldn't contain it. It spread from the sclera to one optic nerve and then the other. Seemed to like the sensory nerve cells. They fought it for two years, but eventually...the risk of infection spreading to the brain became too great, and they removed both optic nerves. I lived. We're not to the 'level' of transplanting optic nerves or replacing them with robotic implants. The end." She turned and put the bread in the warmer.

Titek clasped his hands again. "But...how can this happen? A simple infection? Surely Earth has long known—"

"We've had antibiotics for two centuries. Two centuries of indiscriminate use. It got out of hand in the Thirties—as a result of limitless free energy following the cold-fusion breakthrough. Global mean annual income soared and universal health care became a reality. Too fast. Misuse of antibiotics on a planetary scale for twenty years gave the bacteria of the world a lot of chances to develop resistant strains faster than we could counteract them. By 2050, traditional antibiotics were useless. A lot of people died. It took another fifteen years for the genetic engineers to design drugs that could knock out the bacterial enzymes by blocking their active sites, making it impossible for the chemicals they act on to bind, and effectively killing the bacteria. I was born in 2049."

"I am dumbstruck." Titek rose from the stool and then sat back down. "This is terrible! I cannot imagine...." He brought his long index finger to his lips. "My study of your language is proved insufficient. I do not know the proper thing to say."

"Try, 'hard luck.'"

"I am aware of this expression. But is it not inadequate given this very serious personal misfortune? Would it not indicate a dismissive attitude?"

Aisha shrugged and picked up a block of feta and the knife. "It depends on who you're talking to. With someone like me, it might indicate that you realized I didn't want anybody feeling sorry for me;

that I didn't want to feel sorry for myself. It might even be a compliment."

"I see. Well, then, 'hard luck,' Dr. Thanau."

"Not really." She brought the knife down into the cheese. "In fact, it's the luckiest thing that ever happened to me. I never would have gotten into paleography if I'd had my sight."

"This is a paradox, is it not? That you became an expert in the visual arts of reading and writing though you could not see?"

"Hardly." She went to the refrigerator and took out an earthenware pot. "In a way, all of my studies have been driven by my desire to find alternative forms of visual data input. As a teenager in the Sixties, I was frustrated by the text-to-speech technology then available. It was highly developed but cumbersome and noisy. And the Braille system, the only touch reading system in use at the time, was completely out of date—already two hundred years old." She put the pot in the upper rack of the warmer. "I wanted something better—something that extended beyond the 'canes and dots technology' as I dubbed it in my first book...something that simulated the act of seeing—or even surpassed it. Eventually, that led to my work in artificial sensory data input. I don't normally use my sensystem in the house. If it had been on, I wouldn't have walked into your suitcase."

"Sensystem?"

"Mm hmm." She licked a bit of cheese from her forefinger and held up her hands. "There are micro-transmitters in each of my fingers that send out low-energy EM waves. The feedback—size, shape, distance, color—is processed by a chip implanted in the back of each wrist, and transmitted as galvanic impulses to a neural-sensory net imbedded in the skin of my upper arms. Now it's on...." She touched her left wrist with her right forefinger. "Now it's off. It takes a while to learn to interpret the sensations of pressure, heat, and pattern as distance, color, shape, and so on, but eventually it becomes second nature. At normal resolution, I can 'see,' if you will, not only well enough to keep from walking into a wall, but well enough to tell one tree from another by its shape, or one house from another by its color. Day or night. And I can zoom in to get a higher resolution...." She brought the tips of her fingers together. "Well enough to see that you are wearing an earring in your left ear, and to guess that it is green. There are limitations, I don't mind admitting. Range is one—for example, I can't 'see' the stars—the high res only works on close objects. But I can see printed words. It's not perfect, but it's infinitely better than anything that ever existed before. Of course, the joke is, what with the advances in medical science, only a handful of people need it now." She touched the controls of the warmer.

"But this is robotics." Titek's eyes left her hands and moved to her face. "I understood your work was in ancient texts!"

"I've done both. My work in sensory enhancement grew out of my earlier studies in paleography." She leaned back against the counter and crossed one foot over the other. "You don't see the connection? No one ever does. But it always made perfect sense to me. As a girl I felt that in order to understand written communication well enough to find a nonvisual alternative, I had to study it; go back to its beginnings." The aroma of fresh-baked bread and lentil soup rose from the warmer. "Coincidentally, the oldest extant writings from Sumer and Egypt are engraved in stone or cut into plaster tablets, which meant that I was able to study them first hand. Literally. It didn't matter that I couldn't see them—this was a field where I could compete on a level playing field. As it happened, I excelled. I was an expert on cuneiform and hieroglyphic writing systems by the age of twenty. I was informed, when I started to study applied communications technology, that I had a 'novel' approach. Some people preferred the word, 'childish.' Either way, no one took me seriously. It was good fun watching them eat their words when it worked."

Titek raised a hand. "May I ask a question?"

"Of course."

"Forgive me for going off a tangent, but I am overwhelmed with excitement. You just now used the word 'extant.' This means 'still existing?'"

"Yes."

Titek's tenor voice fell to a whisper. "Am I safe in concluding that your words imply that examples from the period of Earth's earliest writings still exist?"

"I told you you'd find your research fruitful. Of course, the major sites are in Egypt, Mexico, and Iraq, but I can give you a taste of what's to come right here in Greece, which played perhaps the most important role—"

"I am...rendered speechless." He put both hands on his narrow chest and bowed his head. "On my world, scholars can only guess at how the art of alphabetizing began. It is my lifelong dream." He raised his head, excitement shining in his eyes and ringing in his voice. "Tell me...the earliest scripts, were they alphabetic or syllabic?"

"Syllabic."

"Ah! I knew it!" Titek clapped his hands together and bounced up and down on the stool. "Quickly, Dr. Thanau. You must tell me quickly if these early systems utilized pictographs or abstract symbols?"

"What do you think?"

Titek closed his hands into fists. "Pictographs? Which then were rendered over time into abstract symbols?"

"Obvious," said Aisha.

"Haaaaa," said Titek ecstatically. "Oh, I cannot wait to see the examples you speak so feelingly of!"

"In that case, why wait?" She strode quickly from the kitchen and he bounded after her. In the front room, she took her seat at the console. "Pull up a chair." She waved a hand in the air above her head.

Titek looked around and spotted the chair Herman had sat in three weeks before. He hurried to fetch it.

"I don't collect artifacts," Aisha was saying. "I'm a conservationist these days—have to be in my line of work, or there wouldn't be anything left for the next generation." Her hands fluttered over the double bank of keypads at the center of the console. "But...I've got the next best thing."

Titek pulled the chair to her side. He ran his eyes across her console, and tilted his head to one side. "There is no viewer."

"Right. Not a high priority for me."

"Oh, of course not."

"But there is this...." She pointed at a flat slab of white polymer beyond the keypads.

He looked at the grid marked out its surface. It was about half a meter square—and it was beginning to glow.

"This was an early invention," said Aisha. "It's a spatial imager. I sold the patent a few decades ago—still keeps me living in style. The sensystem is more complex, but as I said, it has no market.... The technology behind the imager will not impress *you*—obviously. But perhaps the images will."

The surface of the imager began to rise, and take shape, and then texture and color.

"Sumerian cuneiform. Third millennium BCE. Recreation of a wooden board coated in plaster."

Titek held his breath. Within seconds, a perfect three dimensional reproduction of a cracked plaster tablet appeared, covered with triangular impressions that danced in dense formation across the surface.

Aisha touched the side of the tablet, and a beatified smile softened the hard lines of her face. "There...."

"Is it permitted to touch?"

"Of course. That's what it's for. I developed the technology to help me read inscriptions—that's how I got involved in the high-tech end of sensory science."

Titek's hand trembled as he touched the tablet. He ran the tips of his fingers along the rows of little indentations. "This is extraordinary," he whispered. "I don't have the faintest what it means, but the feeling I get from knowing there is meaning here, hidden in the patterns, is tantamount to euphoria. The reproduction...it is accurate as to size, color, and texture?"

"Naturally. The original is in the Baghdad Museum, and they won't let you near it." She put her hands back on the keypads. "Here's another one. You'll like this."

Titek's face fell as the gray tablet dissolved. But in its place appeared a slab of limestone, in which hieroglyphs had been carved and painted in bright colors.

"Ohhhh," he breathed.

"Luxor. Thirteen hundred BCE. Verses from the Book of the Dead." Aisha's fingers traced out the symbols. "'I have become a spirit in my forms, I have gotten the mastery over my words of magical power, and I am adjudged a spirit; therefore deliver ye me from the Crocodile which liveth in this Country of Truth.'"

"The Book of the Dead," he whispered. "The very name is so

very...alluring. People, so primitive, yet driven to record their story for posteriority. Dr. Thanau." He slapped his hands on his knees. "I must learn to read these symbols. I must! Can you guide me?"

"Certainly—if you want to go to that extent. I'll loan you a portable reader. I've got everything you need on computer. Ancient Egyptian.... Chinese.... Mayan.... Sumerian.... Take your pick."

"I'll learn them all! Oh, Dr. Thanau. I will not sleep a blink tonight!" He touched the spatial imager again. "It is like being a witness to the moment of creation."

"Once you've knocked off the early stuff we'll move on to the Phoenician revolution—the phonemic alphabet, which finally reached common currency some three thousand years ago—about a hundred kilometers from here."

"Is it possible? So close? I am so close to the location of such a monumental event?"

"Your lucky day—although I must add the caveat that there are several dozen other places around the world that claim to have been 'first.' But it doesn't really matter. The development of writing was clearly inevitable. Let me show you an example from the Western Hemisphere. It is a much later period, but the system bears all the same characteristics...."

He drew his chair closer as she manipulated the keypads, while the aromas from the kitchen dissipated and eventually faded away.

Ω   Ω   Ω

As always, Aisha sat at her console—but for once she was not thinking about the patterns of her work. Instead, she reflected upon the patterns of her life, and especially upon the early days of her career, before she had turned to bioelectronics.

From the moment of his arrival, the flame of Titek's enthusiasm had cut through the crust of her later years and reminded her of a time when she too had seen every new discovery as a species of magic. In her youth, she had traveled throughout the Mediterranean and the Middle East, tracking down the secrets of past civilizations in pursuit of her inner vision. There wasn't a book she hadn't read, a scholar she hadn't spoken to, or an ancient site she hadn't crawled through within a thousand kilometers. It had always been easier to work out some tricky problem if she was familiar with the locale, as if the geographic context—the angle of the sun, the local vegetation, and the terrain—were essential pieces of the puzzle. Such adventures she had had...before she had been "discovered" and her eccentricities edited and repackaged for the consumer market; before the luxury of R&D financing in the field of communications technology had pulled her in other directions.

The late morning silence was broken by a soft atonal humming from the other side of the front room. She twisted her lips in amusement. Titek, singing to himself again as he worked.

She had set him up with a server, peripherals, and the commercial version of her imager—slower than the model she preferred, but had a more user-friendly interface. Titek had created a low-frequency link between his own data processor—a small flat box that, when opened, had neither keypads nor viewer—and the server. For two days they had worked together, during which time Titek had familiarized himself with both the equipment and the parameters of his study. In his spare time, he had swallowed Egyptian hieroglyphs (hieratic and demotic) and Sumerian cuneiform whole, and moved on to ancient Greek without pause. By the third morning, he was working completely on his own...and humming.

Some time later, the humming ceased. "Dr. Thanau."

"Yes?"

"There is a reference here to a Nineteenth Century book on the decipherication of the Rosetta Stone, but I can't seem to locate the citation in your otherwise remarkably comprehensive bibliography."

Aisha slipped her toes into her sandals and stood. She needed a stretch, anyway. "Who's the author?" Coming up behind him, she bunched her fingers together and pointed them towards his viewer. It was almost impossible to read letters on a backlit viewer with her sensystem—but sometimes she could make out enough of the shape of the words to get an idea.

"P.R. Delarouche."

She chuckled. "Ah. His descendants hold the copyright to his books and have refused to allow publication for the last fifty years due to some feud with the Université du Paris."

Titek swiveled his head around to look at her. "This is a crying shame, as I feel certain his work would shed light on the phonotactic differences between the scribal and colloquial writing systems in the Greece of that period."

Aisha straightened up. "Come with me." She turned and went up the stairs.

Titek, by now familiar with her abrupt transitions, rose without comment and followed.

She led him to the room at the far end of the upstairs hall. It was filled from floor to ceiling with yellow storage containers, stacked one on top of another.

"I've got to organize this place some day...." She pulled a box from the top level and popped open the lid. Reaching inside, she pulled out a dark, rectangular oblong object and handed it to Titek.

He looked at it with polite interest. "What is this?"

Aisha sat down on one of the boxes. "Open it."

Titek's fingers sought a button, or a latch of some sort, without success. But in the process of turning it over, the casing moved. He slipped his fingers between the pages, and the object fell open in his hand.

"Ah! An ancient script you have not told me of! Or...." He rotated the object 180 degrees. "Oopah. That's better. What do you call this device?"

"A book," said Aisha. She pulled another one out of the box, and ran her hand down the spine.

"Really? Of course I know the word. But I'm not sure I understand. I thought 'book' referred to written works longer than about thirty-five hundred words."

"That is its common metaphoric definition. But originally it referred to what you are holding in your hand. Books were the preferred print medium for fifteen hundred years. My parents loved books—they were born long enough ago to have thought the world lost something precious when the book went out of fashion."

Titek raised his eyebrows skeptically. "Really? Curious. I must say that in shape, color, and design I have never seen anything so distinctly lacking in lovable characteristics."

"No? But surely the Negami had something similar at some point."

He held the book up and looked along the spine. "We have no

record of ever having used such a data repository. It is a quaint concept, if bulky. I suppose it was an awkward but necessary stage in paleographic developmental, destined for an obscure footnote of history now that its questionable usefulness has ended."

Aisha's chin jutted. "It's a symbol of knowledge to the entire human race! Books may be obsolete now, but without them, and the rapid spread of information they made possible, humanity would still be in the Dark Ages."

He held the book upside down by its covers. "It is curious, the importance you place on the container, rather than the idea—or the words that communicate the idea."

"Oh, excuse me. I only spent five years working on that 'container' you're mauling." She snatched the book from his hands. "How 'quaint' of me to think that meant anything."

Titek looked up quickly. "I have unwittingly offended you. Will you forgive my indefensible ignorance? Just because my peculiar interest lies in writing systems does not mean that the media are not of equal fascination and importance in the hands of those more knowledgeable than I."

Aisha fluttered her fingers. "Nothing to forgive. I may be a little prickly on the subject. My first husband was anti-book."

"Might one ask, if it is not too personal a question, why?"

"He believed that anything that hadn't been converted to digital media was worthless. For him, print books were a relic from the period of human barbarism. Now that you mention it, I realize he was more concerned with the packaging than the content. To him, digital books were obviously superior; the embodiment of intelligence and science. You could never prove him wrong, because he refused to read anything that wasn't digital. That sort of rigid adherence to principle became extremely irritating after a while."

"I understand you! Who knows where such a myopic attitude might lead? Please consider me duly chastised. I am sorry to have associated myself with this repugnant philosophy and I applaud you for divorcifying the swine tout de suite!"

Aisha scratched her chin. "He divorced me, actually. Not that I blamed him, since I was cohabiting with my second-husband-to-be at the time. It distressed him—my first husband—that I would do such a thing without bothering with the legal formalities." She cleared her throat. "But perhaps your people also feel that the, ah, legal niceties should not be so lightly dismissed."

"No indeed. We are...a self-indulgent race. Our laws are few. I will go so far as to say that we have been astonished to find your Earth culture so preoccupied with form and rules. But we try to understand that this is a tortuous stage of development through which you must go. Meaning and expression are the elements that enrich life, and form is merely a tool with which to deliver them where they are most needed. For a time this distinction is blurred; later on in your history, you will allow the stream to take precedence over the channel again."

"That's encouraging." She pulled another book from the box, and hefted it in her hand. "A bit ungainly, isn't it. You're right, of course. The book is just a stage in an ongoing process. In fact, I admit I only print a few hundred of each of my books, out of respect to my parents, really. Readers find it frustrating not to be able to search or manipulate printed text. Not to mention how irritating it is to discover a typo. In a digital text, you just correct it, but in print, you're stuck with it."

Titek seated himself on a box. "What is 'typo?'"

"It could be a mistake in data input that escaped the notice of the proofreader, or a spelling error."

"What is 'spelling error,' in this context?"

"A deviation from the conventional order of letters in a word, resulting from ignorance or accident." Aisha pushed at her hair. "Before the printing press, there was no such thing as correct spelling, or spelling errors. Today, people are horrified by spelling errors, as if spelling mistake could compare with getting your facts wrong. Another example of my species stressing the packaging above the content, I guess."

"If a mistake in spelling is a matter of sufficient importance to arouse disapprobation, why do you not, as the Chinese did, adopt a wholly phonetic alphabet, which will naturally reflect speech?"

"Because we've never found one that works. And I assure you, we've tried. I've tried myself! The problem is, even though we all speak English, we speak it with different accents around the world—

different phonemic systems, I should say.... But you talk as if...."
She fingered the book in her hands. "Have your people developed a viable phonemic writing system?"

"Ahem...." He raised his eyebrows and pursed his lips. "That introduces a touching subject. A writing system...it can be considered a tool, can't it? A creation of a society?"

"Obviously. We do not emerge from the womb with pencils stuck behind our ears."

"You cannot know how much it means to me to hear you speak so incontrovertibly." He put his hand on his chest. "And yet...can you imagine your life without the pencil; without the written word?"

"No. Everything would be different—what I do, what I care about. I would simply not be me. But that doesn't mean I'm not perfectly aware that people lived hearty and happy lives before the written word or the pencil existed."

"Then you accept that the cultural invention of writing has influenced the development of your species as much as the biological process of evolution?"

"Or more so." She handed him the volume she had been holding. "Here is my first book. Somewhat idealistic—I was young. The topic is the effect of a fully developed writing system on social structures and conventions."

Titek received the book from her with a ceremonial bow and opened it to the title page.

"So your people have a phonemic writing system?" asked Aisha again.

Titek turned a page and smiled. "I like this: 'I have carried away the darkness by my strength, I have filled —'"

She reached out and closed the book over his finger. "You didn't answer my question. Twice."

He rested the book on his knees with a sigh. "I must choose my words carefully. And I am not accustomed to this exercise.... You see, to say that writing is a tool is to say that writing is a form of technology. As you know, I am prohibitioned from sharing our technology with you."

Aisha scowled at the floor. "But surely you are not prohibited from discussing your writing system in general terms? I did not ask to see it, I just asked about it. For example, we know you have the technology of interstellar travel via spacecraft. You will not, of course, tell me about that technology. But would you hesitate to tell me whether the craft had windows, or what the space rations tasted like?"

"There is no prohibition on discussing such things. The sixty-four-dollar question is, where do we draw the line? We have a certain...guideline, based upon long experience, that when dealing with a less-advanced culture, it is better not to mention certain social and technological developments. For your sake, not ours."

"That sounds paternalistic to me. Do you have the right to decide for me what I want to hear?"

"It is a complex issue for unsophisticated minds and hard to explain without appearing to condescend."

"You're already condescending. But don't worry—it's one of the perquisites of a superior intelligence and experience. I am frequently accused of condescending."

"Oh, no! Dr. Thanau! I find that impossible to believe! You are always so very gracious with me. But...perhaps I can use that as a metaphor." He sat with his knees close together, looking straight ahead, while he gestured with one arm. "If you were able to travel away back in time—not to the age of the Pharaohs or the Mycenaeans, but to a far-off time before even simple metal alloys had been fabricated, or the wheel invented...."

"We call it the Stone Age...."

"Ah! It is a highly evocative language, this English, capable of both high frivolity and pithy moments, though you may resent its usurpation of your mother's tongue. So. If you had a time machine that allowed you to travel to the Stone Age to study the ancient humans, and to live among them in their caves, you would not give them a pistol, would you?" He made the shape of a pistol with his hand.

"Obviously not."

"Nor would you allow them access to your time machine?"

"No."

"However, if you had a heating device in your cave to warm your toes on nippy nights, you would allow them to gather round it, too, wouldn't you?" He held his hands out, as if warming them by a fire.

"Yes."

"But you would not bother to explain how it worked, because you would know they could not possibly understand the principle of cold fusion, correct?"

"Correct."

"And you would make notes using your computer, and not bother to hide it from them, because they could not possibly get past a simple 128 bit encryption, let alone understand what they would find there?"

"Very true. Forgive me for interrupting, Titek, but so far all of this is an argument in support of my position that you should answer my question."

"Attend. You would not tell your Stone Age friends, whose average life span was twenty-five years, that in your day, people regularly live past the ripe old age of one hundred, would you? Or that the roaming buffalo they killed and ate was in your time a protected species, and that anyone harming the beast would face legal recrimination? Or that their blackened nails and missing teeth would be considered ugly and unacceptable in your society? Or that the paintings they drew with charcoal on the cave walls and considered a feat of power and wisdom, would one day pale beside the work of Mr. David Roberts, let alone that of the ancient Egyptians whose art so inspired him? Would you?"

"No."

"And as it would be with you and the Stone Age peoples, so it is with me and you. The moral of the story is, that to raise some subjects without a shared frame of reference is only opening a can of worms. Capisce?"

"Perfectly. But I put it to you that we do share a common interest about writing systems. Why can't you answer a simple question? Is your writing system phonemic?"

Titek sighed again. "You are a darned persuasive advocate. I find myself powerless in the face of your rhetorical skills, not to mention the breadth of your knowledge. Very well. I will spill the beans. No, our writing system is not phonemic—in the sense that you mean. Because the truth is, we do not write to represent the sound of our voices speaking words at all. In fact, writing as a form of communication is unheard of on my world."

Aisha frowned. She heard the truth in his voice, but the words carried no meaning. "I don't understand."

"Nor would your Stone Age friend understand if you explained how a few hydrogen atoms embedded in a lattice of certain isotopes can give off heat."

"That's not what I meant," said Aisha impatiently. "It is axiomatic that technical advances are interwoven across the scientific disciplines, and do not occur in isolation. On Earth, the ability to write was the prime facilitator of science; the release mechanism. How could you possibly develop the other sciences...travel across the galaxy, if you did not write?"

"I beg your pardon. I have fallen back on the very cultural stereotypes I have dedicated my life to breaking!" He opened the book again, and touched the paper reverently. "I did not say that we did not depend on writing in the past. Indeed, I am here because I am sure we did. It is just that...writing has become as obsolete on my world as the cuneiform has on Earth. Consider this point, Dr. Thanau: just because writing is an inevitable cultural development for your species—so inevitable, as you have told me, that it occurred in several places at different times as societies advanced at different speeds—why would you conclude that it is the only such development that will occur? What makes you think that an even more effective communications tool will not some day appear, as your society continues to advance, when you have the tools available to create it?"

"I don't...." Aisha stopped and turned her head. She was suddenly in uncharted intellectual territory, groping for the pattern. "I never looked at it that way. I've never looked to the future for the answers...only to the past."

Titek's voice fell to a whisper. "What if I were to tell you that the written word, this tool of sentience we study so fervently, is in a certain sense a hindrance to communication, not an aid?"

A corner of Aisha's mouth turned up. "You would not be the first to have noticed. Three hundred years ago, Talleyrand said that language was given to us to conceal our feelings, not to express them."

Titek's hand flew to his breast. "Truly?"

"Truly. But we take language—oral and written—as the best, if not the perfect, choice."

"Ah! The best choice. That is the crux of the matter. Words are delightful playthings; so essential for wit and grace; so attractive to the quick mind. But sometimes, when something important is happening, they are only a distraction, and what is really going on lies unspoken beneath the surface words." Titek tapped his finger on the book. "For such times, there is another choice, another tool, which to my people is as essential to life, to our understanding of ourselves, as writing is to you."

"Which is…?"

"I can't explain…."

"Because it is too complex for my Stone Age mind to understand?"

"Not at all…." He looked at her hands, and at the comm loop that dangled forgotten from her ear. "You are poised on the doorstep of discovery."

"Then try another metaphor."

"I will give it a whirl." He held the book to his lower lip and raised his eyes to the ceiling. "I have learned from you that writing on Earth started with the pictograph to represent the idea. The ideograph, it is sometimes called. This, as I have seen, was 'improved' by the invention of abstract symbols that represented syllables, and then by the phonetic alphabet. But—in a certain way, the pictograph is closer to the thought, is it not? Because it portrays the idea itself, instead of the word for the idea. What if…there were a way to reach back to the pictograph…to the thought itself."

For an instant Aisha sensed the pattern, but she could not put words to it, and it fled from her mind's grasp. "I can't quite…see it."

"This is expected. Could your Stone Age friends picture your spatial imager, no matter how heroically you tried to describe it to them?"

She shook her head and sighed.

Titek sighed. "I fear you find my condescension oppressive."

Aisha turned to him with a laugh. "No, I assure you, I do not! Tell me, does this advanced communications technology have anything to do with direct computer-to-brain transmission, via neurostim technology?"

"I must not talk in such technical terms."

"My question crosses the line. Forgive me. And...thank you! You've given me much to contemplate—although perhaps I should not admit that."

"I was fully aware of what your reaction would be."

"You read me like a book." She took the volume from his hands and put it back in the box. "And now.... I brought you up here to find that Delarouche, didn't I?"

"No kidding? You have his work in print media?"

"An autographed first edition."

"Once again you lead the way. I now begin to feel the magic of the book! 'Autographed first edition.' I can hear in your voice that this is a thing to be proud of. I cannot wait to hold it in my hot little hands."

"Good. Because I have no idea which box it's in."

Titek looked at the jumble of yellow boxes, and his mouth dropped open.

Ω   Ω   Ω

"The sun is the color of red raspberries; the sky behind it creamy yellow streaked with blue. The water has turned silver now—except for where the sun nears it and is reflected on its surface—and it is completely still. A sailboat comes into the harbor. The two ribbons of its wake trail behind it, close together at first, then spreading wider until they disappear in the glittering silver sea."

"How many sails?"

Titek took a swig of beer from a green bottle. "Two."

Aisha breathed in through her nose, then exhaled.

They sat on the green bench overlooking the marina, a small table cluttered with bottles and the remains of a cheese board in front of them. Aisha, her sensystem off, listened to the sounds of the dying day, enjoying the subtle changes in temperature and wind that accompanied the sunset.

"The rim of the red sun touches the horizon. The surface of the water is on fire. The sun sinks quickly." He paused, one minute...two. "It is gone now. The sky darkens. At the zenith it is a deep blue; to the east, beyond the mountain, it is night."

"Beautiful." Aisha sighed. "When you describe it, I can see it like a picture in my mind."

"Dr. Thanau.... I hope this does not infringe upon a taboo subject, but I admit that my curiosity—" He brushed a fly away from the cheese. "I would say sympathy, too, but I do not wish to offend—is aroused by the idea of a life lived wholly by words, without images."

"You mean, what's it like, being blind? I'm not sure I know." She lifted her hands and fluttered her fingers in the air. "Though technology has its limitations. I can read about a mountain, and, because in my youth I saw mountains, I can get an idea in my head what it must look like. But it's different with things I've never actually seen. For example, though I've read a description of you, without being able to actually see you, I can't really know what you look like."

"Would you trade your ability to read for the ability to see?"

"No." She cut a sliver of cheese. "The word may only be a symbol for the idea, as you say, yet I am far better off not being able to see the thing than I would be if I were unable to use the word for it."

"You state a deep truth," said Titek.

"Do I? Then it is a cold truth. Because there are times when I think nothing can replace the sight of the shore at dusk, or sunlight on a garden. However, now is not one of those times. I find it unusually satisfying to hear your words. Through them, I share with you the pleasure of seeing a new world."

"It impresses me that, although your sensystem is off, you instantly know what I am describing, even when I do not know what it is myself."

"You are an unusually precise speaker."

"Do you think so?" He put his elbow on the back of the bench. "No, you are just being gallant! I'm sure I make many bungles in my attempts to describe the spitting image of what I see."

"A small percentage only, I promise. And that is because you are so dedicated to using the full scope of the language. Ah! don't deny it, I know it is so."

"I will not deny it, Doctor. I am flattered beyond belief that you notice and approve. But let me test your confidence in my ability to describe. What is this...this...creature, or thing, that sits in a shell-like container and drags itself along the stone patio, leaving behind it a trail of...slime?"

"A snail."

His large eyes grew immense. "Good heavens! This cannot be! I...I don't understand."

"What?"

"I fear to betray a confidence, but Mr. Herman described you to me as being 'brutally honest and hard as snails.' I assumed from the context that he referenced some creature that was strong and invincible...but this insect is...eeaa...mushy."

Aisha's lips worked overtime. She ran a hand over her face. "Nails. Hard as nnnails."

"Ah! Once again I am enlightened by your willingness to explain the intricacies of this dad-burned English language." He sighed. "Idiomatic expressions are very difficult to use properly. It is at such times that I feel most alienated from your culture. There is much to see and learn beyond the confines of my work." He sighed again, and popped a piece of cheese into his mouth.

Aisha tapped at her bottle with a forefinger. "I'm afraid I haven't been helping matters. I've let you coop yourself up from dawn to dusk for a solid week. Probably because I don't get out myself much any more. I'm afraid I'm not much of a host; never was. Don't know how to treat people, I guess...." She raised the bottle to her lips.

"Treat me as you would any visiting foreigner. This is the recommended strategy in low-to-medial cultures that are still infected with elements of tribalism masquerading as national pride."

"All right. Then, what do you say about going down to the marina and taking a look around? You learn more about what you're studying if you take in the scenery."

"But this is so true!" He swiveled around to face her. "It is for this reason that we insist on remaining incognito during our field work! To suck up the atmosphere!"

"If you really want to go out in the field, I can take you to some of the ancient sites, so you can get an idea of how the people who used the early scripts lived."

"Is it possible? I would like that more than anything!"

"Well, then I'll organize it. It'll take me a day or two.... But tonight we have the sights and sounds of Kimolos! Let's go." She rose.

"Now?" There was astonishment in his voice as he rose to follow her. "But we have made no plans, laid no groundwork! Is it not too late in the day to begin an expedition?"

"If we leave now, we'll be back by midnight and you can still get a good night's sleep."

"Is it safe to be out at night?" His voice dropped. "I don't want to get smuggled."

Aisha blinked twice, twitched her lips, and made a titanic effort at keeping her mouth shut before succumbing to a burst of laughter that leaped fountain-like from the region of her heart.

Titek stood with his hands folded across his chest until she stopped. "Did I say something funny?" He sounded a little hurt.

Ω   Ω   Ω

"You have not locked the door."

"There is no lock." Aisha checked again to make sure she had put her debit chit in her shoulder bag. "Thanks to that obsession with the past you once mentioned as being characteristic of my species, the tourism trade is booming. Thus the good residents of Kimolos are shockingly well-off, and the penalties for petty crime extremely harsh." They headed down the first flight of stairs. "Are you worried about your belongings being stolen?"

"My suitcases are locked, and my data processor cannot be accessed without a voice and palm print. And I'm carrying my communications pack with me. But still...."

"We haven't had a theft for thirty years."

"Thus my timidity about staying out past midnight is unwarranted."

"You are as likely to turn into a pumpkin as be robbed."

He stopped. "Pumpkin? I fear...."

"Never mind. Just doing a little informal test of your knowledge base."

"Ah! I hope I—oops!" He caught her arm as she stumbled.

"Thanks." She steadied herself with a grimace. "The rustic look is good for the tourist trade, but these picturesque lanes are a pain in the ass if you can't see very well. I don't get enough detail unless I stare at the ground, which is as monotonous with a sensystem as it is with eyes."

"Is it appropriate to offer you my arm?"

"Well...." It had always been a point of pride with her to walk alone.

He bowed slightly and extended his arm. "I promise I will not succumb to either oversympathy or a false sense of superiority."

She wavered a moment, then shrugged. "In that case, why not?" She slipped her arm into his and they headed down the second flight of stairs.

In fact, she noted approvingly, he did not support her at all, allowing her to keep the contact as light as she liked. No wonder she never went out by herself; having an arm to lean on was much better than stumbling down the mountain alone. In fact, it made the walk through the quiet night quite pleasant....

"Dr. Thanau, I find I have so many questions about these exotic surroundings."

"Then you'd better ask them."

"I fear their simplicity and number will be a source of irritation to a sophisticated woman such as yourself. Is it not true here, as on my own world, that it is impolite to bore your host to death with a series of mundane questions?"

"Certainly. But you are a tourist—more or less—and I expect you to ask questions, and will steel myself against any serious discomfort. It is true I dislike to play tour guide. But in this instance...." She waved her free hand in the air. "My patience is increased in proportion to the distance you have traveled to visit my homeland."

"Ah! I am greatly relieved. I am so anxious to know why the houses are painted such bright colors?"

"There is a long tradition—"

He jolted to a halt and sniffed the air. "And what is it that smells so sweet?"

"That is the scent of orange blossoms. Do you see the tree by the blue house?"

"Yes! And.... Oh! Do I not see fruit on the tree, as well as blossoms? How can this be?"

"It is a peculiarity of some of our citrus fruits to blossom and bear throughout the year."

"Incredible. Such a beautiful metaphor for the cycle of life! And what is the significance of the cross on top of the white building with the spire?"

They sauntered down the hillside, Titek chattering happily and Aisha indulging him with polite and informative answers, pitted by only the occasional barbless bolt of sarcasm.

Ω   Ω   Ω

The marina by night was an alluring arcade of towering boat masts topped with twinkling lanterns on the one side, and busy shops and restaurants overflowing with customers on the other. Titek and Aisha were just two more faces in an anonymous crowd, out for a stroll along the boardwalk. Attracted by the music, they joined a circle of tourists watching a pair of dancers and a balalaika player. Titek was soon swaying and holding his hands over his head with the rest of the crowd, while Aisha stood at his side with an indulgent smirk on her face.

When the music stopped, Titek joined in the enthusiastic applause, and gratefully accepted a flyer from the young girl in bright red attire who sped through the crowd handing them out.

Titek raised the flyer to the level of his nose and put a finger to his chin. "They are traveling performers, who seek to uphold the time-honored traditions of Greek folk culture." He held the paper to his breast and sighed. "To see such an example of a primitive lifestyle takes my breath away. And their clothing...it is so extremely evocative of a simplistic agrarian culture!"

A departing member of the crowd bumped into Aisha, and she sent a dirty look in his direction. "It's a show for the tourists, really."

"It is? To me it seems more authentic than I could have ever imagined!"

"Yes, well, I'm sure they'll sell you an authentic replica tambourine if you like. Or give you one for free—if you buy the music crystal."

"Really? I would so like.... Where do I...?"

Aisha leaned against a mooring post while Titek went to buy a crystal from the balalaika player. When he returned, she put his package in her shoulder bag for safekeeping. Then she steered him toward the north end of the marina, where the fishing boats were docked.

The further out along the boardwalk they rambled, the fewer people they saw, and the quieter the night grew. Soon they were aware of the creaking of the boats and the slap of water against the jetty. Titek's questions became sporadic under the combined spell of the darkened water and the black shadow of the mountain against the sky.

Aisha was also content with the silence. She had always loved walking through the warm sea breezes, listening to the sounds of the harbor and smelling the salty, fishy smells. But how long had it been since she had come here? Of course fighting through the crowds by herself was so tiresome....

When they reached the end of the boardwalk, they sat for a while on a white bench, contemplating the sea, both lost in their own thoughts and sensations, neither interested in speech. Only when the mosquitoes arrived did Aisha decree that they head back.

It was late by the time they re-entered the commercial area, and the crowds had thinned, or been absorbed by the restaurants with their colored lights and tiny tables. The smells of Greek cooking were everywhere.

Aisha smiled and drew in a deep breath. "Skordaya."

"Sorry?"

She stopped and turned to him. "How would you like to sample some authentic Greek cuisine? We'll sit, drink coffee, and have a light supper."

Titek eyed the clusters of little tables with their white tablecloths and flickering candles with the look of a boyscout contemplating a liquor store. "I suppose it can't do any harm."

"I haven't been here in years." Aisha raised a hand and moved it from left to right. "But one of these cafés used to have the best fresh-baked bread on Kimolos." She moved her hand up and down, and then closed her fingers. "This one." She grabbed hold of Titek's arm and pulled.

Ω   Ω   Ω

Time did not pass on Kimolos, and Aisha was greeted by the staff of The Herakles as an honored sister and ushered to the best table in the house—which to Titek's uninitiated eye looked exactly the same as all the other tables, although it did command a good view of the trio of musicians entertaining the customers.

"You are a visitor to our island," said the maitre d' as he settled Titek into a low chair.

"How can you tell?" asked Titek, trying to hide his disappointment.

"You have a certain air of the foreigner. We know these things. I guess you are from...England?

"Not quite." Following Aisha's lead, he picked up the large linen table napkin and placed it in his lap.

"Eire, then. The land of the leprechaun! Welcome!" He handed Titek a menu. "Welcome to Kimolos, the most beautiful island in the Mediterranean, or the universe! If you need anything at all during your visit—anything," he winked at Titek, "you just ask me."

Titek dimpled under this manifestation of felicity. He started to rise from his seat, sat back down, and gave a little bow with his head. "You are too generous."

"You can start by getting us a bottle of mineral water, some skordaya, and bread," said Aisha. The maitre d' bowed and disappeared. Aisha switched off her sensystem and turned to Titek. "Do you think you can eat garlic?"

Titek poured over the menu, selecting, after much pondering, a dish of grape leaves stuffed with rice, and a seasonal salad. The skordaya arrived, and he, following Aisha's motions, dipped a bit of bread into it, and nibbled a corner. He announced that he thought he could eat garlic, and didn't see what all the fuss was about.

There was a shout of laughter from one of the boats. Titek turned. A louder outburst followed.

"Oh!" he said.

"What?" asked Aisha.

"Several young people dressed in bright colors are having a joyful time on a pretty white boat. They are so funny! One of the boys has climbed the masthead and is hanging upside down by his knees on a crossbar. The others are throwing silly things at him, which he tries to catch. Oh! He has caught the bottle! He takes a drink while upside down. Oops!" There was more silvery laughter.

Aisha smiled and nodded. The musicians began to play, something slow and melodic. Her heart soared. She had always loved Greek music played on the violin.

"Dr. Thanau." It was clear from the sound of his voice that he had a confidence to share.

She leaned forward. "Yes?"

"There is a woman seated at a table by the musicians."

"Yes?"

"She appears not to notice that her blouse is, ah, slipping downward quite immodestly."

Aisha kept her expression as innocent as possible. "Is it an off-the-shoulder blouse?"

"I am not an expert in fashion plates, but...yes, I would say...very off the shoulder. More off the elbow at the moment.... And when she reaches down to pick up her napkin.... Oh, my. Someone should.... Dear me!"

"Let me guess—is she dining with a young man?"

"A very young man...."

"I see. Forgive me, but...you are from an advanced society...yet this sight shocks you?"

"Of course!"

Aisha pursed her lips and raised her eyebrows. "We can go somewhere else if you are embarrassed."

"Me? Embarrassed? Oh, dear me, no. My concern is for this unfortunate woman. She is making a spectacular of herself, a veritable laughing stock. Her friend should inform her of the situation."

"Is she the one laughing loudly, and talking with the American accent?"

Titek gasped. "How did you know!"

Aisha chuckled. "I'm blind, not deaf. Do not fear for her modesty. I'm sure she is well in control of the situation. Tourists visit on their summer holiday, looking for a little multi-cultural amusement. This is a Greek island, you know. We have a reputation to uphold."

"I fear I do not apprehend the significance of this declaration."

"Greek islands are renowned for providing many opportunities for romance."

The waiter swept by and slid half a dozen little plates onto their table. "Did someone mention romance? The gentleman has come to the right place! Kimolos! The most beautiful place in the world! If you need anything at all during your visit, sir, just ask me." He placed knives and forks on the table, winked at Titek, and disappeared.

Titek watched him go. "Everyone is so very nice."

Aisha took a sip of wine. "Remind me not to let you go out too much on your own."

"I don't wish to go out on my own." Titek nibbled one of the grape leaves, and then popped it into his mouth. "The flavors are subtle, but wholesome. In fact, it is all very delightful. A light supper." He waved his fork in the air. "I like the way that sounds. A light supper."

"I'll take you to an Indian restaurant, next time, if you're going to turn out to be a gourmet. There's a fine one in Athens...."

Titek took a sip of water and continued to pick through his salad. "The red one is tomato, and the green one is cucumber. What is the pink one?"

"Scallops."

"Shallops? That is an onion, I think? Shallots? Shallops?" He put one in his mouth. "It has a consistency reminiscent of avocado."

Aisha tore off a piece the bread. "No, it's seafood. Shellfish." She dipped the bread into the skordaya.

There was a sudden silence, following which Aisha learned that some sounds are indeed universal, as Titek's stomach turned, and scallop, grape leaf and garlic alike announced their imminent reappearance.

Aisha grabbed her napkin, and thrust it towards Titek. He snatched it from her, and ducked his head below the table. Aisha listened to a soft, helpless sound, barely audible above the strains of the nearby violins.

A waiter materialized and leaned over Titek's shoulder. "May I help you?"

"I'm afraid my friend has been taken ill," whispered Aisha.

"I'm so sorry," mumbled Titek. There was a tremble in his voice.

"That's all right, sir. Let me escort you to the washroom." There was a scraping of chair legs on the tile floor.

Aisha listened to the retreating footsteps, and to the sounds of

46

the table being cleaned and reset. From the unbroken stream of conversation around her, it did not appear that anyone had heard or noticed.

Ten minutes later, Titek returned and resumed his seat.

Aisha leaned forward. "I'm so terribly sorry," she said in a low voice. "I forgot all about there being scallops in the salad until you mentioned it."

"No, no," said Titek calmly. "These things happen. No irrevocable harm done. Best move on and forget all about it. I knew the risks. When in Rome...." He tried a little high-pitched laugh, then sighed. "It's just...difficult sometimes. I try to remind myself that my own ancestors must have been...omnivorous...a very long time ago. But I must tell you frankly, Dr. Thanau, it does not help. You can study a society in an early stage of development, but you can't turn back your own sociological clock."

"Well I think you do a marvelous job of coping with life in a primitive society! I never would have forgotten about the scallops if it wasn't that you seem to fit in so well, here."

"Really?" His voice brightened.

"Yes, indeed." She nodded firmly when she said it, to add a protective cover of sincerity to the underlying falsehood. "Now, as you say, let us move on. Do you think you would find a cup of coffee medicinal?"

"I think I will stick with water. Perhaps a little bread later on.... But I insist that you continue with your meal. This evening has been too bewitching to bring to a premature end."

"You are a trooper, Titek." And there was no denying that.

He lifted his face happily. "While I was in the restroom, I thought of something I came across several years ago—while I was learning your language and keeping my toes crossed that I might visit your planet. It told of the remarkable adventures of an Earth anthropologist investigating a primitive culture. Her name was Margaret Mead. She encountered many surprising customs that forced her to overcome her personal revulsion and cultural preconceptions. I feel—spiritually—very close to her right now."

"I'm flattered you came to Greece rather than Papua, New Guinea."

"I'll tell you a secret. Until today, I didn't realize there would be any difference." He held his long forefinger to his lips.

Ω   Ω   Ω

For two days Titek remained in the close embrace of his studies, absorbed by the mysteries of an obscure Mycenaean script that had puzzled more than one scholar down through the centuries. Aisha fed him a steady diet of bibliographic cross-references and pasta salads, both of which went down smoothly and seemed to energize him for the task at hand.

For her part, Aisha spent her time—when not acting as chef or reference librarian—making arrangements for an expedition to the island of Delos. This entailed booking transport and carrying out subtle negotiations with the Greek Ministry of Antiquities for permission to visit areas closed to the public for her "visiting colleague."

Consequently, ten days after Titek's arrival, the two of them made their way down the mountain at the crack of dawn, took the service tunnel from the marina to the air field, and boarded a shuttle for Delos. Following a short flight and speedy disembarkation, they headed for the center of the island—a flat-topped hill accessed by a winding footpath.

Delos is a small island, less than four square kilometers in size, uninhabited but for the archeological teams that come and go with the seasons and a year-round governmental presence to operate the Tourist Information Center. Aisha led the way past the ruins of the ancient port, around the Sacred Lake and up the stark gray hillside. The land was littered with broken bits of stone columns and scattered gray blocks. But the way upon which they walked was smooth and modern.

It was noon when they reached their destination and stood at the crumbled gates that marked the entrance to the Temple of Apollo. Titek looked out from under his wide-brimmed hat at the field of ruins before him. What he saw were more gray stone blocks, some faced with white marble, others broken and scattered among the sunburnt grasses. Here and there the roofless walls of an ancient building rose head high, or a lone pillar towered above them. There were no trees. Just a field of stone—through which a handful of tourists crawled—and the gray-green sweep of the hilltop beyond.

"This way," said Aisha. She pulled him off the smooth walkway and onto a path paved with uneven flagstones.

Titek hitched the picnic basket he carried higher onto his arm. He hurried as fast as he could, but Aisha went even faster, fairly pulling him along.

When they came to the top of a little rise, she stopped. "There," she said.

He came to her side, then froze in his tracks. "Oh, my." His grip on her arm tightened.

Aisha nodded to herself in satisfaction. Although she couldn't see them, she knew they were there—nine stone lions, tall and muscular, guarding the way to the sanctuary with open mouths in which the echoes of mighty roars still lingered. The Terrace of Lions, it was called, quite rightly. She moved forward—and, perforce, immediately back. For although he didn't pull against her, Titek stood as fixed as stone himself.

"What?" she asked, a little annoyed.

"They are—bigger than I thought they would be. And...so lifelike."

"Not at all. They are considered very stylized. Real lions don't have such long torsos and necks." She tried to move forward again.

"Real...?" He was still rooted in place, but she felt him twisting to look over his shoulder. "The lion is not a mythistical beast?"

"No. But there are no lions in Greece—or anywhere in Europe. In fact, there are very few left in the world outside of zoological reserves."

"I am glad to hear it. Our scouts said there were no dangerous beasts on Earth—but...since coming to Greece my confidence in their reporting abilities has wavered."

"You're quite safe." She felt the muscles of his arm relax. "From living dangers. However...." She pulled his arm closer to her side and lowered her voice. "I must warn you that the lions were placed here twenty-five hundred years ago by the will of Apollo. For Delos was his birthplace, and to fulfill the promise his mother made in return for the safe delivery of her son, he gave the lions magical powers to protect the Isle, that it might never be defiled by alien intruders."

"Ah!" He matched her tone. "Then I must hope they do not see through my disguise." He pushed his sunglasses up his nose. "Fortunately, I mean them and their temple no harm. This is indeed a place of great power and majesty."

"Yes. Even though I can't really see it, I can feel it. Speaking of which...." She removed her hand from his arm. "Come. There's something I want *you* to see."

Holding her hand ahead of her, fingers poised as if holding an invisible egg, Aisha stepped off of the pathway and walked to the nearest lion. Titek followed her more slowly, turning his head from left to right as he stepped through the scrub grass and rubble.

She stopped in front of the lion and stood motionless.

He came to her side, and gazed spellbound into the beast's open mouth. Up close, he could see that twenty-five hundred years of weather had pitted the stone and removed whatever facial features the beast had had.

"There's an inscription on the pedestal," said Aisha. "A verse against trespass. In ancient times, written words were thought to carry a special power. They were used to ward off evil. We call them curses, or spells, and don't pay much attention to them, today."

Titek put the basket down and knelt in front of the lion. Parting the curtain of yellow grass, he looked in silence at the carved letters thus revealed.

A breeze blew over the crest of the hill, and Aisha turned her face and let it cool her brow. It smelled of the sea.

Titek reached out a hand, then paused. "It is permitted to touch?"

"I did, my first time here."

"But you were not an alien to these shores. I do not belong here, and I do not wish to waken the wrath of the guardians."

"Ah! But you are in no danger of that! You are my colleague and my guest. According to all the ancient traditions of this land, it is my duty to protect you from harm; to provide sanctuary for you as you travel far from home. Nothing can hurt you as long as you are with me."

He ran his fingers over the stone, tracing out the symbols. "Miraculous. This is an extraordinary experience. It is not only the spell of the writing, or the majesty of the lions. It is the sense of time passed; of being pulled back to one's origins—which is passing strange, because these are not my origins. But the parallel history exists, as I knew it would. It is thrilling. It is overwhelming. It is humbling. Yes, that is the word. Humbling—in a way that my people can never experience. Only now do I fully understand what a tragedy that is."

The wind swirled, and Aisha turned into it again. "You have no ancient ruins on your planet?"

Titek shook his head. "We have examples of our architecture from the past, yes—but to us it is not ancient."

"Is twenty-five hundred years a shorter period on your planet than on Earth?"

"No." He looked up at the lion's stout forelegs and burly chest. "I was not using years as the measure." He touched the lion's paw. "It has been many thousands of your years since my people were at Earth's present level of technological development. And so much time has passed since we were at a level that compares with the builders of this temple that we cannot even guess at it."

Aisha stirred restlessly, and turned to him, holding her hair away from her face. "Am I following you? I know you said you hadn't had a writing system for so long that it was an anachronism, like a spear would be to me. But...are you saying your civilization is so old that there are no extant examples of your pre-technological society at all?"

"Yes."

"But you must have copies, or records of some sort?"

"No." He rested a hand between the lion's ears.

"I find that incomprehensible. More than anything else you have told me! Wouldn't there be artifacts? Are there no museums?"

"There might be if—" Titek looked along the row of lions. Only the haunches remained of two of them, looking like urns with long feet resting upon empty pedestals. "If we still lived on our planet of origin." He put his hands on his knees and stood.

"I see." Aisha ran her tongue across the backs of her teeth. "How long ago did your people, uh, emigrate?"

Titek took Aisha's arm. "When these statues were newly carved, we had already been on our adopted home five thousand years." He picked up the basket, and led the way back to the main path.

They walked past the lions, toward the Temple ruins.

"I don't get it." Aisha shook her head. "How did you come to study early writing systems if you didn't have any examples?"

"Until now, my work has been wholly theoretical. Until now. I did have access to the research of colleagues who had visited two other societies about a thousand years ago. But both those societies were far more advanced than yours, in the late-medial period, with a single language. I beg your pardon if...."

"Don't bother, please."

"Yes. From that research, I was able to see some scattered examples of what were purported to be early scripts. Unfortunately, those cultures had no tradition of archeology or anthropology, let along epigraphy, and so remained largely in ignorance of their own history. Both were proud of their disinterest. They did not share the passion for the past that characterizes your society."

"Then what did you base your work on?"

"On my own world, I was restricted to philological data—and passages from our early literature that mentioned the subject. I had my breakthrough when I managed to incorporate a mathematical abstraction of our earliest art forms, images of which have been preserved, into my work. This brought me a certain celebrity in the halls of academe. My work was considered very new and provocative—and that is unusual in a scientific tradition as old as ours."

Aisha pursed her lips and blew through them. "I guess there aren't many corners that haven't been scoured out after five or ten thousand years of research...."

"Not many."

"It's a wonder your society manages to maintain any interest in the sciences at all, considering how slim the possibilities for original work must be."

Titek was silent.

Aisha turned her head. "Am I showing my low-to-medial lack of sophistication again?"

"No! No.... Just the opposite." Titek came to a halt just outside the ruined walls of the Hall of Dolphins. "Dr. Thanau, I find I must share my darkest fears with you—in the hope that your perspective will aid me in the difficult time to come. Is this asking too much of our short acquaintance?"

The textures of emotion were strong in his voice. She squeezed his arm. "Of course not."

"Then let us sit on this convenient outcropping of Mesozoic Era igneous rock so that I may tell you my story." Titek put down the basket, pulled a plaid handkerchief from his pocket, laid it on the rock, and sat. Aisha hiked herself up beside him.

"There is a great burden upon me, Dr. Thanau. It is terribly important that I succeed with my research. My 'government,' as you would call it, is counting on me, and has moved heaven and earth to afford me this chance."

Aisha raised her eyebrows. "I thought the Negami only sought knowledge for its own sake—to discover something new in the universe—because you had already studied yourselves to death and were desperate for virgin territory. Is that not true?"

"My people do not lie, Dr. Thanau. It is indeed true that, for ten thousand years, our expeditions to other stars have been motivated by a passion for discovery alone. We have shunned planets in the primitive period of development for fear of tainting that which we wish to see in its native state. We are scrupulous about leaving the planets we visit in the same pristine state as we find them. This is our way. However, in the case of my research, there is—for the first time—an additional reason. A reason of importance to the future of my people."

Aisha ran her fingers along a fold of her galabeya. "I admit I can't guess at the connection between paleography and politics in an advanced society."

"Never fear, I will explain." A strong gust of wind ran along the hilltop, and Titek put a protective hand to his hat. "If it lasts long enough, a society may indeed achieve a high level of…sophistication. But experience tells us that what is true of society as a whole is not necessarily true of each and every individual in that society. By which I mean that while it is true my society is more technologically advanced than you can wildly dream of, it is equally true that its individual members are as capable of rank foolishness as the biggest Tomfool jackass in the galaxy!"

He looked out upon the ruins with worried eyes. "In fact, the truth is smack dab as you have stated it. Interest in science—in what you call the scientific method—is indeed waning on my home world. I regret to say that many of my people are so ignorant of their origins that they have lost their moorings in the safe harbor of reality, and are rudderless upon the bosom of the sea of history, drifting farther and farther from the proven ways that have let us live in peace and harmony for millennia."

Aisha pulled at her earlobe.

"I see the skepticism on your face, Doctor. You think I am making a mole hill into a mountain, but I assure you I am not. There is a subversive element on my world. It grows stronger every day. It has no name, but those who feel its presence, and its insidious pressure to conform, call its followers the Zealots. Under a mantle of spirituality, these dunderheads are spreading illogic and superstition across the width and breadth of our society. Their influence is a dark cloud of ignorance. They take pride in our science and technology without understanding it; without realizing that it is not miraculous, merely extremely technical. Attend. Because we have found no society older than our own, they assume that ours is the oldest, and that because it is the oldest, it is the first, and because it is the first, it is the best. Worst of all, having convinced themselves of their superiority by this sophistry, they greet an opposing viewpoint as a personal attack."

"But this is just simple stupidity!" burst in Aisha. "How is that possible in an advanced society? Don't you have schools? Don't you have science requirements?"

"We do have schools, and we certainly study the sciences. But those of us who even notice something is wrong do not know that answer. Did we make a fundamental error; turn down a wrong path? Our 'lifestyle,' as you would call it, is very luxurious. We enjoy a high degree of comfort with very little stress. Some sociologists say that Zealotry is an inevitable outgrowth of a society that has had no serious conflict for so long it has utterly forgotten what horrors it leads to."

"But...need it lead to horrors? Earth has had its share of fanatics—why, there are people in every country who will tell you that the end of the world will come with the end of the century in four months time. Most of us ignore them—or laugh at them. Can't you just ignore yours?"

"That is what we have always done. But the centuries have crept by, and the Zealots now represent a plurality on my planet, and are beginning to pressure the scientific community."

"How?"

"By discouraging research—or even discussion—on topics that are contradictory to their belief system—which is, I must say, a wildly improbable concoction of snuff and nonsense."

Aisha turned to him in sudden realization. "Are you one of the ones they are putting pressure on?"

Titek sighed unhappily. "Yes."

"That's ridiculous! How could the study of script origins threaten anybody?"

"They believe I pose a serious threat to their doctrine. And in fact I do, for if I am successful, it may be possible to end their preeminence and turn my world away from the path of destruction the Zealots have put it on."

"How can you do this?"

"Dr. Thanau, since I have met you and come to appreciate your knowledge and perspicacity, I have been struggling with a dilemma. I know I should not tell *you*—a representative of a society just at the beginning of discovery—so many of the gory details. But, even as you are surprised to discover such stupidity on my advanced world, I am surprised to find such insight and intelligence on your primitive world. I did not expect this. And—" he nodded to himself, "it is not in my nature to swim against the tide—metaphorically speaking, of course, as I do not know how to swim—of opportunity. I feel sure in my innermost heart that if you knew what I am trying to do, you would be able to help me to the fullest, whereas if I keep you in the dark, I might miss my chance for success. So—I am going to tell you more."

He settled back on his igneous rock, dangling his feet in the air. "The Zealots have invented a specious creation legend out of smoke and mirrors, in complete contradiction of such historical records as do exist concerning life on our planet of origin. They believe our people were created by God during a supernova five thousand years ago, and that we are the manifestation of her perfect vision. They take for granted the technology upon which their comfortable lives depend—literally, for they take it as a gift granted them from God. In a nutshell, they claim that when God created our people, she also created our technology, our cities, and the arts and sciences. Our ancestors presumably woke up one morning to find the whole kit and caboodle set up for them. Shazam! We are supposedly the descendants of God's first children, the true heirs to a life of ease and bliss. In their own eyes, they can do no wrong. Our mission—I kid you not—is to provide a model of blissful social behavior for the rest of the galaxy."

Aisha ran a finger across her upper lip.

Titek frowned. "You are silent."

She sniffed. "I'm not sure what to say."

"You fear to offend."

"Perhaps."

"You have no need of such a fear."

"All right. Then—I've got to tell you this is one of the silliest things I've ever heard. I mean—seriously! Your people are smart enough to travel from star to star but are still capable of producing nincompoops stupid enough to believe such a fish story?"

Titek's face dimpled. He watched her shifting irritably on the white rock beside him, the embodiment of earthly scorn and ridicule. He raised his face skyward. "It is refreshing to hear the objective opinion. It was worth the length of the journey to hear it. Thank you, Dr. Thanau."

Aisha barely heard him. "You can't possibly consider these people a real threat. They sound like they couldn't do anything for themselves. Let them try to run things their way. The first time the ion dishwasher breaks and they need it repaired, they'll find out which side their bread is buttered on. Surely it's just a fad!"

"Would you want your world run by those people I have heard you refer to as the 'religious whackos?' Would you risk having them deconstruct your society—your technological advances of the last thousand years—on the bet that it was just a fad?"

She thought about it a moment. "No. Okay, I take your point. Even without the technological deconstruction, too many people's freedoms would suffer."

"You have hit the nail on the nutshell."

"So just where do you fit in."

He touched the tips of his fingers together. "The Zealots' doctrine precludes the possibility that there was ever a time in my people's history when writing did not exist—not to mention a time when the more advanced communications technology I once told you about did not exist. If I can show by analogy that writing and communications systems are not created whole, but develop step by step over time from an oral tradition, it will help prove that the creation myth is untrue. If I can even show that literacy is an inevitable development of sentient life on many planets, it will prove that our culture is not in any way unique in that regard. This might be enough of a kick in the pants to force our history back on its proper track."

"Hmm.... We are talking about people who believe that when God created the Negami he created—"

"She...."

"She created the computer, et al., to allow them to communicate?"

"Yes."

"Out of the womb with a pencil stuck behind the ear?"

"Yes."

Aisha twisted her lips to one side. "You have an uphill task."

Titek nodded. "We hope to convince the more enlightened to start with. In any attempt to introduce a new idea, it is a mistake to approach the hard core element."

"True. Titek. I find this incredible. Are you sure...sure that your society so strongly parallels that of Earth? Because I'm finding it hard to believe that the world I know could ever collectively be that blind. I know you've all had some sort of surgery to pass as human, but...."

"The physical differences between our species are minor. A certain scaliness where our bones are close beneath our skin, one or two calcareous outgrowths...." He ran a finger along his jaw. "But in terms of philosophy, I assure you we are like two peas in a pod. That is the paradox!"

He looked around the hilltop, and out to the sea. "Whatever the mystery of the universe; whatever natural law decrees that sentience shall be accompanied by two arms and legs, a head, and fingers with which to carve the symbols in the stones you have shown me—whatever the ultimate meaning of life, I do not know. More importantly, I do not need to know. I am happy not knowing. It is enough for me to see—as you have shown me in the purposeful development of simplicity towards complexity in Earth's writing systems—the meaning, the direction, at work along its slow but inevitable path. Indeed, do we not presuppose a 'direction' when we speak of our parallel experience? For how could our experiences be parallel, if they did not have a direction in common? This 'direction,' this 'way,' eternally sought, followed, lost, and sought again amongst the peoples of our universe, is a more meaningful symbol for me than any illusion of perfection. For is it not true that in a universe in which everything is known, in which everything is perfect, God herself becomes meaningless?"

He shook his head. "As for the foolishness of the Zealots...how can I laugh at them when I see the danger they represent. You find them incredible. But are your people so different? Can you or anyone on Earth imagine a life without your computers, your books, your Plex? Yes, your society is young enough so that, intellectually at least, you accept that there really was a Stone Age; a time when there was no writing. But emotionally—do any of you feel it? No. The tool has become at least as important as the user. You cannot imagine that it was not intended to be so. You look upon someone who cannot write as an anachronism. You cannot speak when born—although of course you have the biological capacity to do so. A child raised in isolation will have ideas and feelings, but will never speak. It is society that provides the words for the feelings and idea. Language is a tool of civilization, not of biology. Yet when you meet someone who cannot speak, you think of him or her as inhuman, do you not? Subhuman; deficient; diseased. Is it such a big step for you to consider that, after ten thousand years, my people would consider life without their technology counter-intuitive, and—foolish sophistry—conclude that it was never so?"

Aisha gazed out over the terrace. Though she could see nothing, she could hear the breeze rustling the grass, and the drone of a tour guide on the other side of the temple. She could tell when the sun ducked behind a cloud, and she had a feel of the size of the place from the background echoes and air currents.

"No," she said at length. "It is not such a big step. People are capable of thinking anything the imagination can stretch to."

"Exactly. Dr. Thanau, I am indeed lucky to have made your acquaintance. And now that you know the real purpose of my study, I hope to be able to proceed lickety-split with even greater focus. It is a great relief for me—I am...not used to keeping secrets. I do not feel so far from home...so alone, now."

Aisha picked at a loose piece of moss on the rock.

"You speak with your mission regularly, don't you?"

"Yes, but they are either explorers or pencil-punchers. They do not understand.... You are the only communications expert I know within sixty light years, Dr. Thanau."

"Then I'm glad you told me. I'm sure we'll be able to make progress working together. Only...I wouldn't tell Herman and his people about this if you can help it."

"Never fear. It is true that our people cannot lie. However, we do not tell everything we know. But...you do not mind keeping this from him?"

Aisha snorted. "I don't owe Herman anything, or his government. He was my student once, and for some reason I don't understand, he admired my work—or maybe it was my unambiguous approach. I don't know. He went to work for the US government right out of college—good riddance."

"Did I not read in your Who's Who entry that you worked briefly for the US government yourself?"

Aisha stiffened. "For about six minutes. Herman recommended me as a consultant about ten years ago when they restructured the old Internet into the Plex. Unfortunately, I didn't pass their security clearance. Ridiculous circumstances. They accused me of professional impropriety.... Me! As if antiquities had anything to do with the Plex anyway!"

"I'm sorry."

"Don't be. It was a mistake to even consider the job—the last time I ever let myself get flattered into doing something I didn't want to do.... Politicians are all alike." She turned to him. "Which is why I must ask you—are you absolutely certain your mission views your work with the same importance as you do?"

"There can be no smidgen of doubt."

She pushed out her lower lip with her tongue. "Herman told me your proposal was last on a list of fifty."

"Yes, the position of honor." He laid his hand on his heart. "I feel the responsibility greatly."

"I see." Aisha nodded. "Well, Titek. There's something else your scouts missed. On Earth, we prioritize from top to bottom, with the highest at the top. The Commissioner would never have okayed your work if he had suspected it had special significance to the Negami mission."

Titek straightened his back. "I am shocked to hear this extraordinary revelation. We assumed my proposal was chosen as a way of rewarding our long years of patience and good will!"

"They chose you because they think your field of study is so obscure no one could possibly object to it, and...." She hesitated.

"Continue, please."

"Well, to be blunt, they think you're a harmless eccentric."

"This is most strange. I had thought, from reading your popular literature, that as an alien visitor, I might instill fear in those I met. Tell me, am I so...non-threatening?"

"Your manner is very self-effacing," said Aisha. "And I would call you...fastidious."

"Really?" Titek removed his hat and patted the wisps of hair behind his ears. "At home I am considered to be quite aggressive and adventuresome; I have been told on more than one occasion that I am...unconventional."

Aisha scratched the side of her nose.

"Of course," said Titek, with crushing humility, "I must realize that in a frontier society, I cannot compete for machismo with the local yahoos."

"Well, never mind. Looks can be deceiving. It's time to go—that tour guide is coming our way and I refuse to listen to the inaccurate nonsense he's going to tell his group. I have a spot in mind for our picnic—away from the tourist trails. It has a lovely view—they say. After lunch I want to show you the sanctuary for alien gods on the other side of the hill. Maybe you'll meet someone you know...." She stood up, brushed the bits of rock and debris from the back of her legs, and took Titek's arm.

Ω   Ω   Ω

They followed a faint trail that threaded through a valley dotted with shrubbery and rocks and wound up the side of a steep hill. Titek stepped carefully to avoid the goat droppings. The trail disappeared at the foot of a grassy slope, up which they walked, heading toward the lone olive tree that grew at the top. The hot sun drew sweet smells from the ground cover, and insects buzzed among the wildflowers.

When they reached the shade of the tree, Aisha pulled a Mylar blanket from the basket, and spread it on the ground. Kneeling, she pulled a bottle of wine and a couple of glasses from the basket. She breathed deeply of the fresh mountain air and raised her hand to see where Titek was. "It is traditional to sit on the blanket when picnicking."

But he stood looking westward over the harbor.

"What?" asked Aisha.

"It is beautiful. The colors...."

"Tell me." She sat back on her heels and held out a glass of wine.

He took the glass from her hands. "The grasses of the meadow are the same color as the leaves of the olive tree—I see pale green and iron gray, and silver in the sun. There are tiny yellow flowers peeping through the grass. The meadow slopes toward the sea, gently at first, and then sharply, making an edge over which I cannot see. But in the distance I see white boats with white sails approaching the harbor...."

Aisha nodded.

"And I see flying things in the air! Like giant mosquitoes; they seem too fragile to be birds. What can they be? They have long bodies and translucent wings. They fly in circles, thirty...fifty of them."

"Dragonflies."

"They are beautiful." He sat down beside her on the blanket. "They are dancing in the sun. Their wings are blue and silver, and they sparkle. Now the sun goes behind the clouds, and everywhere the colors deepen. Your world is beautiful. You are beautiful."

Aisha chuckled as she rummaged in the picnic basket. "And you said you didn't know how to lie."

"This is not a lie!"

61

"Then you must be judging by standards I am not acquainted with. Or perhaps physical beauty is not important on your world?"

"Not for long-term relationships. Fortunately for me."

"Do I conclude that you are both unattractive and in a long-term relationship?" She handed him a plate of tyropita.

"For the second, the answer is no—how could I be when my life is dedicated to intensive study on distant shores? I was speaking theoretically. For the first, you must judge for yourself."

"As you know, I am not able to get enough detail with my sensystem to form a useful opinion."

"You can scan me with your imager when we return to your cottage, if you like."

"I could. But—" Aisha switched off the sensystem and pulled herself closer to him. "Why don't we do it the old-fashioned way?" She reached out a hand towards the sound of his voice.

Titek looked at her hand, hovering just in front of him. He looked at the lines of her face, like carved marble weathered by sun and wind and rain. He put down the glass and curled his fingers around her wrist, placing his thumb against her palm.

His touch was gentle as the quick pat of a kitten's paw. It guided her hand to his face and abandoned it there.

The chin was pointed, the skin smooth. She drew her fingers along the angular line of his jaw toward his ear; there was no hint of stubble or even of hair follicles. The ear was small and shell-like, the little earring that pierced the lobe quite snug. She raised her other hand and touched the sides of his face with her fingertips; the cheeks were plump and soft, the cheekbones not prominent. The nose was long and pointed; a good sturdy nose above a long, deeply dented upper lip. She ran the forefinger of each hand up the sides of the nose and onto the ridge of the eyebrows; the bone was round and covered with feathery eyebrows.

"Close your eyes," she said.

The eyes were deeply set, large, and close together. The lashes were long, like a child's. Her fingers fluttered across his bony temples, lingering until she felt his pulse begin to quicken. The forehead was high and broad, the skull rather bumpy. There was a patch of soft hair behind each ear, running around the base of his skull.

"You forgot my mouth."

"I was saving it for last." She placed the tip of one finger on his lips, softly, like down falling onto a pillow. The mouth was small but full—little bud-like lips that smiled beneath her touch, although he had been motionless before.

"It tickles," he said.

She lowered her hands. "Not exactly an Adonis, no—but a good face, a scholar's face." She folded her hands. "A little boyish. One wouldn't mistake you for a man of action. Of course, I'd have to examine the rest of you to make certain."

He moved closer to her and lifted her hands from her lap. "Go ahead."

She hesitated only a moment, then reached out and touched his neck. It was thin and long. She slid her hands to his shoulders. They were bony beneath his cotton shirt. She ran her fingers along his collarbones, and then downward. His chest was thin and narrow, his stomach flat and smooth. She hesitated again, acutely aware that his breathing had deepened. She cleared her throat. "I'd better stop. I wouldn't want to cause any embarrassment."

His voice floated out of the darkness. "Embarrassment is a social plague specific to the transient developmental state of civilized beings, associated with low-to-medial cultural clumsiness. It does not exist in either primitive or advanced cultures. I have noticed, however, that you show no signs of this trait."

"I must be ahead of my time," she said. "But to state it more directly…I don't want my investigations to lead to the commitment of a cross-species offense."

"Why would a scientific interest in an alien species offend me?"

Her fingers played with the buttons of his shirt. "I was thinking of something more unconventional…say, adventuresome or aggressive…than a purely scientific interest."

"A healthy curiosity is also a cracking-good thing."

Smothering a smile, she freed the first button from its moorings. "Perhaps I am too vague."

"Not at all." He brushed her wayward hair from her ear and neck. "I am an expert on all forms of figurative language, including double entendre, innuendo, and polysemousness."

She undid the second button. "I'm glad to hear that, because clear communication is very important for mutually satisfying collaborative research." She brought her face close to his chest. His skin smelled of jasmine.

"Then I propose the following topic for your consideration...." He touched his lips to her ear. "That: words have a strong power of arousal in the hands of the expert."

The last of the shirt buttons undone, she placed her hands on his stomach. The skin was soft and warm. "I concur. Which is why I must be very careful in your presence." She slid her hands around his waist.

His fingers fluttered along her arms. "I fear you flatter me. You must know I was talking about you."

She raised her head and looked at him, and pretended she could see him. He brought his mouth to hers and kissed her lips, softly and without urgency. She kissed him back, putting her hand behind his neck to pull him to her.

High above, a seagull turned its wings against the breeze, swooping down the steep hillside toward the shore. Its far-off cry broke the silence of the day. The wine bottle fell over and rolled unnoticed onto the grass.

"Please allow me to assist you," said Titek. "The buckle tends to stick. I fear this belt was not my wisest purchase, but I was so smittened by the image of the pony...."

The sun came out from behind the clouds, making the grass of the mountain top glow like burnished gold. The light sparkled off the wings of the dragonflies as they danced above the wildflowers.

"Oh my!" gasped Titek. "Yes, that's.... Oops! And for you...? Is it permitted to touch? Ah! This is all very enlightening. There has been much speculation about the possibility of mutual gratification in cross-species—"

"Shut up," she said, muffling his words with her lips. Together, they canted sideways onto the blanket.

The breeze blew harder, sending a napkin skipping across the grass and causing the branches of the old olive tree to creak. The leaves shivered, making a rustling sound. In the distance, the blue waters of the Mediterranean rippled silver in the sun.

"Ah!" said Titek. "Oh…! Yes, it is true what you said, you are my sanctuary. Nothing—"

But suddenly she pushed him away and sat up.

"*Gamoto.*" She hiked her galabeya down below her knees. "I can't do this."

Titek sat up too, a startled expression on his flushed face. He clutched his shirt flaps across his narrow chest. "Oh! You find my skin texture too coarse. I told our surgeons that your species—"

Aisha shook her head. "No."

He placed his hands on his cheeks, holding his pointed chin between them. "I have let my boisterous exuberance run away with me in a selfish manner, and have been unwittingly insensitive to your physical needs."

"No!" She stood up, switching on her sensystem.

He stood up too, hopping on one leg as he pulled up his trousers. "You are experiencing a sense of professional guilt due to the cultural impropriety of engaging in sex with a colleague."

She cut an X through the air with both hands. "Shut up!"

He buttoned his trousers and folded his arms across his breast. "Then it can only be that your high moral scruples have overcome your personal desire."

She stared at nothing, breathing heavily through her open mouth. "I…." She shook her head quickly. "Leave me alone, will you? This has nothing to do with you. No, that's not true. But I…. I need to be alone…to think." She stooped to gather the picnic things, but could not find the utensils, which had slid off the blanket. "Oh, hell, you bring the damned basket!" Snatching up the blanket, she turned and trudged across the sun-sweetened meadow, fingers outstretched before her.

Ω   Ω   Ω

Titek hunted in the grass for the utensils and castoffs from their interrupted picnic. He found his sunglasses under a napkin, and put them on. He packed the basket, taking care to secure the wooden flaps by joining up the little hooks and eyes on either side. Such a quaint method of closing something…. Straightening up, he was surprised to discover that one of his shirt tails was hanging down a hands-breadth below the other. Shaking his head, he unbuttoned the shirt, realigned it, and buttoned it up again, correctly. Then he put on his hat, picked up the basket, and walked slowly across the grass away from the olive tree.

He located Aisha at the bottom of the little valley. She was sitting on the remains of a Doric column, her lean forearms resting on her knees. In her hands she held a blade of grass, which she shredded until there was nothing left of it. Then she plucked another blade of grass, and shredded it, too.

"Please to say the word when you've completed thinking," he called out.

She raised a forefinger in acknowledgment.

Titek pulled his plaid handkerchief from his pocket, spread it on the grass beneath a tree, and sat.

Ω   Ω   Ω

Half an hour passed. Titek relocated his seat as the shadow of the tree crept eastward.

Ω   Ω   Ω

Finally, Aisha stirred. "Okay, I've completed thinking," she called.

He went down the hill toward her. She moved over, making room for him on the column.

Her spine was ramrod straight, her voice firm. "The only way to say this is to say it." But then her mouth sagged and tears gathered in her eyes. "I've done a disgraceful thing."

"This small episode? Uncomfortable perhaps, and, eeaa...well. But not disgraceful!"

"I'm not talking about that." She ran a hand across her mouth. "I've known Bobby Herman for fifteen years, and I've never liked him. But I agreed to spy on you for him, to help him steal Negami technology. The truth is the only reason they let you come to Greece is because they thought you were an easy mark. They thought they could manufacture an opportunity—"

"But this is understood!" Titek raised his shoulders and spread his arms. "There is no need to tell me this! We expect to be subjected to clandestine attempts by less-advanced species to pilfer our tech-

66

nology. This is small potatoes!"

"Just—wait. What you don't know is that Herman and his people are in my cottage right now, going through your things and uploading whatever information they can out of your processor through—"

Titek made a clucking sound. "They will not succeed. They must have my palm print, and the physical key, which I carry with me at this very moment, as well as my voiceprint speaking the password."

"Will you—please—wait to respond until I've told you everything?"

Titek touched his fingers to his mouth and nodded.

"Thank you." Aisha pressed the heel of her hand against her forehead. "The imager I showed you is only a backup. The real one, the high-res scanner, is so big I had it built into the structure of the house for stability. Your workstation is in the center of the area I have set up for high-res scanning. I left it on for days with you sitting right in the focal point. I got a scan of your hand for the palm print, and a scan of the key. I also recorded your voice giving the password. There's a record of everything you did, every move you made. Now...." She grabbed his forearm. "Tell me that's nothing!"

Titek made a little O with his mouth.

She let him go and hunched forward, her head hidden between her shoulders.

Titek looked up at the blue bowl of the sky. There was not a cloud to be seen, now. He looked across the valley to a stand of olive trees. Their delicate, almond-shaped leaves glistened in the sun. He looked down at the cracked and pitted marble of the ancient column upon which he sat. Grass grew in the cracks of its stained surface.

"Aren't you going to say something?" mumbled Aisha, without raising her head.

He looked at her. "Why do you choose to tell me this?"

She laughed sarcastically. "Don't you think this is something you should know?"

"Curious expression.... How can I quantify what I 'should' know? My question is about you, not me. What I wish to know is why you tell me this now, rather than earlier, or later, or never?"

"Because I realized—quite suddenly—that what I had agreed to do was terribly wrong. That miserable dog Herman made it sound so reasonable, he—"

"Why blame Mr. Herman? It has been only an hour since you assured me you would not reveal our conversation—"

"That was a separate issue!" She raised her head and straightened her shoulders again. "That was between you and me, as colleagues, as...as.... I would never betray a professional confidence. Besides— Herman has no interest in writing systems, or in Negami politics. He wouldn't care or understand about the Zealots. He only wants your technology. You must not believe that I was pumping you for information to give to him!"

He pushed at the air with his hands. "Reassure yourself that I do not believe such a thing. But neither do I understand the difference between spying on me in the one instance, and keeping my secret on the other."

"I just didn't think it would hurt anyone if Herman did a little snooping. It sounded like an intellectual game, the way he described it. Just picking up stray bits and pieces, hints and clues—things you might let fall without even noticing. No one would be hurt. No one would notice."

"But if that is true, why are you upset?"

"Because when I held you like that I saw—oh, God." She wrapped her arms around her stomach and rocked forward. "I saw that what I had done wasn't a game, or harmless at all! Because it was *your* voice print I had taken, *your* key I had scanned, *your* belongings Herman's people were going through. Don't you see? You were a guest in my home, which should have been a sanctuary—but instead I made it into a laboratory for studying you. You were my colleague, whose opinion I had learned to trust and respect, whose respect and trust I wanted. And I saw...all at once...that I could never have them, because I had already betrayed you!" She turned her face away from him.

"Then it is the developing intimacy that creates the distinction? If we had remained mere acquaintances...?"

She shook her head. "What I agreed to do was disgraceful, no matter who I agreed to do it to. But, yes, it must have been the intimacy that opened my eyes to the truth. I thought of you for the first time as a part of me...." She breathed in shakily. "I guess you were wrong about me showing no sign of that low-to-medial cultural clumsiness. I have never been more embarrassed in my life."

"This is not embarrassment; this is shame. Shame has no limit in time or space that my people know of. It is truly universal."

She bowed her head.

"Well." Titek took off his sunglasses and cleaned their lenses on his shirt tails. "No use crying over split milk. Let us move on. We must see what luck Mr. Herman has had before we decide what to do next. It could be worse."

"Really." She jerked her head up in annoyance. "I don't see how."

"You might have found my skin repulsive. That is something I am not sure—oopah!"

He tipped over backwards as she gripped his shirt and kissed him. His hand flew to his hat, which he held squashed flat on his head until, a minute or so later, she detached herself and resumed her former position.

"Holy Toledo!"

"Think what you want about me, but don't think that."

"I can safely promise I will not." He flexed his jaw.

Aisha raised a hand to her neck. She had always had unmanageable hair, straight and fine, the type that can find its way out of any bond. She unfastened the clip from the back of her head and gathered together the straying wisps.

The touch of his fingers on her cheek brought tears to her eyes. He ran a hand down her arm and took her hand.

"I've ruined everything," she whispered. "I'm so sorry."

He squeezed her hand and patted it. All around them, dragonflies flew in aimless circles, their green and purple wings glistening in the hot Mediterranean sun.

Ω   Ω   Ω

The cream-colored cottage was bathed in golden late-afternoon sunlight. The yellow flowers, nestled among the leaves of the vines that grew over the windows, had already closed their trumpets for the night. The neighbor's cat sprawled among the flower pots, pretending to sleep.

Aisha opened the door and stepped inside. She held her hands in front of her and looked around, closing and opening her fingers. "I don't see anything," she said. "You look."

Titek tiptoed over to his workstation and unlocked the drawer where he kept his data processor. "Yes," he said at once, "they were here."

"What is it, some sort of motion sensor? Or something that records organic residues?"

"There was a scrap of paper beneath one corner of the processor. It has been moved."

"Cutting-edge," said Aisha. "Herman was right—he has a lot to learn from you."

While Titek took inventory of his files and inspected his equipment, Aisha sat on the stairs, listening to his hums and sighs. There was no further evidence of interference; everything was as he had left it.

"Mr. Herman and his posse were very careful." He wiped his hands on his hanky. "No doubt they have learned much from previous examinations of such processors."

"Really," said Aisha with more unease than sarcasm. "And yet Herman led me to believe they had had no success in getting their hands on Negami hardware."

"Perhaps they have not—we try to avoid learning about these instances. It does no harm. We bring little of real technologic importance into the field, for the obvious reason." He rose from his chair. "I must now investigate my bedchamber." Aisha pressed against the railing as he passed her, then followed him up the stairs.

In his room, Aisha sat on the bed and slipped off her shoes. It had been a long day, and they had done a lot more walking than she was accustomed to. She rubbed her feet while he went through each item in the suitcase, one by one. It took a long time. Then he opened the second suitcase.

When he was done, he sat on the floor with a small white box before him and sighed.

"Did you find anything?" asked Aisha.

"This is what you would call a data crystal—what your parents would have called a book—or a library." He pulled something from the box and handed it to her. "The ones I have here are mostly personal, but there are a few reference repositories. I brought one hundred and forty two of these with me. I count only one hundred and forty one."

Aisha turned what he had given her over in her fingers. In shape, size, and texture, it was like a plastic playing card. "Are you sure? Maybe you left one downstairs—or in your processor."

"I do not put them in my processor. Nor have I had them outside of this room. Nonetheless, I will check again. Better saved than sorry."

He went through everything a second time, then searched the room, the pockets of his clothing in the wardrobe, the dresser, the night stand. Together they stripped the bed, moved it away from the wall, looked under the mattress.

When they had finished, they stood together in the middle of the room.

Titek clucked his tongue against the roof of his mouth. "There is one missing. I cannot doubt it."

Aisha frowned. There was a defeated quality in his voice. "I can't believe Herman would actually take anything. He stressed repeatedly that he would never do anything anybody would notice."

"I might not have noticed—anymore than you would notice if one of the books from the yellow boxes in the next room was missing—if I had not been alerted to the need to look."

Aisha re-seated herself on the bed. "Do you think he knew what he was taking?"

"I think he knew it was a data repository. But these—what would you call them?"

"Cards?"

"These 'cards' are unmarked—for human senses. So he could not know which one he took."

"Could he open it...read it, do you think?"

"No. Not now. But...it is possible that, over time, his scientists will learn how to do so."

"Is that bad?" She smirked at herself. "Stupid question. How bad is it?"

"It is very bad...though not, perhaps, in the way you think."

"Tch." Aisha folded her arms across her breast. "But it doesn't add up! Herman's plan was set up to take years to bear fruit. He knew that if he did something too obvious, and was found out, your people would take steps to see he never got another chance! It might even mean the end of the Commission, which would be a terrible blow to him. He told me himself—he has staked his entire career on this plan."

"Did you believe him?"

"Yes, I—" She stopped, and jutted out her lower lip. "I did. Why wouldn't I? Why would he lie about that?"

"I don't know." Titek sat for a moment with a forefinger pressed to his lips. "May I ask you to exercise your remarkable memory and relate to me the conversation you had with Mr. Herman?"

"All right." Aisha ran her fingers over the smooth surface of the card for a moment. Then she told the story as well as she could, without glossing over the details. Some things made her uncomfortable, but she kept strictly to the facts.

"Hmm," said Titek when she was done. "I fear that Mr. Herman is more dangerous than I thought."

Aisha nodded. "He is a highly manipulative man. I see that now. He fed my ego; let me walk all over him. Then he got me to do what he wanted."

Titek tapped his chin. "I think even now you do not fully appreciate the epic extent of Mr. Herman's subterfuge."

She nodded again. "He must have known I'd think the chance to meet an off-worlder was too good to pass up, and agree to his plan, even though I knew it was unethical. I thought I hid my excitement, but he must have seen right through me."

"That is not what I mean."

She frowned. "What do you mean, then?"

"To answer that, you must look inside yourself."

She shook her head. "I don't understand."

"Forgive me for presuming to direct you, but this is a moment of extreme importance—not only for you and me, but for the future of both our worlds. You must ask yourself why you agreed to his plan."

"But I've told you...."

"You have mouthed comforting words. Words are not important now. Do not be distracted by them—they are only the colorful package in which the truth lies buried. Beneath the words lie the feeling, the idea...."

"I don't know what you mean."

He came and sat beside her on the bed. "Do you want to know?"

"Yes—of course."

"No, there is no 'of course.' But if you want to know, then look deep into yourself and allow yourself to feel again what you felt that fateful day when Mr. Herman visited you. Turn off your sensystem. I will guide you. First, when you waited for him. You felt what?"

Aisha turned off the sensystem. She closed her eyes and thought. "I was curious."

"Why?"

"I knew he was on the CONER Commission. I knew he wanted my help. I couldn't imagine what he thought I could do for him, but I was intrigued. And I was suspicious."

"Why?"

"I thought he might want me to consult on some sort of surveillance operation."

"Once again you prove the depth of your perception. As things have transpired, it would seem that your initial instincts were correct. And when he began to tell you of his plan, were you instantly attracted to it?"

"Not at all. In fact I became more suspicious. I thought he was trying to use me. When he started to talk about shadow plans all the alarm bells went off. I thought it sounded like he was trying to get me into a situation of questionable integrity. He used words that sounded reasonable, but it was quite clear what he was talking about: covert operations. I thought he had underestimated me. Hmm. I'd forgotten that."

"Because then something very important happened. You went from being against the idea to being for it. What was it that swayed you?"

She pursed her lips. "I don't think it was any one thing. He painted it in patriotic colors. I began to think about all the good it would do humanity to acquire new technologies. For a while I was undecided. Then I—" Aisha opened her eyes. Still the world was dark. "No."

"What?"

"He can't have meant that. He can't have read me like that."

"Like what?"

She shook her head.

"You must tell me."

"No, I won't." She switched on her sensystem, and was immediately aware of him sitting beside her, his hands clasped in front of him. "My thoughts are my own."

"Yes, that is what I've been trying to tell you. All that remains is for you to take possession of them by speaking them."

"I can't."

"Yes you can. There is nothing to fear. I already know, I have always known, and it does not change my opinion or feelings for you."

"You're lying." She stood above him, hands and voice trembling. "How could you know?"

"Sh, sh." He stood and took her hand. "You know I am not lying. You caught a glimpse of the truth on the sacred isle of Delos, when you first saw that what you had done was wrong. In your heart, you already know the rest. No? Then I will speak the words for you. When Mr. Herman mentioned the advances that might result from the acquisition of our technology, it occurred to you, as he knew it would, that medical science might be advanced to the point where you would be able to see again."

"No." She took a step back.

He tightened his grip on her hand. "Your pride has never permitted you to face it, but inside you have always felt that you were cheated by an accident of history; robbed of something precious that everyone else takes for granted."

"No!"

"This is why you find it so easy to rationalize your actions—you think that whatever you do to get back what was stolen from you is justified."

"No."

"Yes."

She closed her eyes. "Yes." She pulled her hand from his, and this time he let her go. "Yes. You are right. I've never had a pure motive in my life. I've never cared about anything—only about myself, only about being able to see."

"No." He clucked at her and raised a finger. "That is not so. That is the monster of fear you have created by hiding your true thoughts. You are a brilliant scholar, and have done great good in the world."

"I'm a poor scientist. I let myself accept Herman's arguments without question, because they justified what I wanted to do."

"Your motivations are no less complex than anyone's, and more noble than most. Although in this one area of your life you have been unable to face the facts, in all other areas you are a shining example of unselfish devotion to the discovery and dissemination of truth for the betterment of humanity."

"Do you think so?" She clenched her fists. "Well I think I have intentionally fostered a reputation for being brutally honest to keep people from looking close enough to see my flaws."

"Perhaps you appear that way to others. But to me, you are the only human being I have met with whom I can be myself, because you are the only one who seems to see and speak the truth."

Aisha's brow wrinkled, and her shoulders sagged.

"Come, let us attempt to put this into perspective." Titek sat on the bed and patted the pale blue cover. "Do you think you are the first to go down this path? Do you think I have done nothing in my life I am ashamed of? Why, I have fallen flat on my face more times than I can stake a shiksa at! These are the trials your life has brought you. So what if you stumble? Are you perfect? Do you want to be? Is the universe perfect? How many people in your shoes would have had the courage to have this conversation? I will save my approbation for the occasion upon which, once having seen the error of your ways, you err in the same fashion again. Until then, I will continue to admire you as a woman of great wisdom, unlike anyone I have known in this galaxy."

Tears gathered in Aisha's eyes. "Oh, Titek...you're such a liar...."

He smiled at her. "Better, now?"

She nodded, brushing away her tears. "But there is still one more truth to face: I've ruined your work."

"I have not said so."

"I can hear it in your voice...."

It was Titek's turn to sag. "Well...I admit that the road ahead is looking like a rocky horror."

They sat in silence for a little while, and outside darkness fell.

Eventually, Titek stood and turned on the pink seashell lamp.

Aisha watched as he sat on the floor and opened a suitcase. "What are you doing?"

"I must communicate with my mission. And I must tell you, I greatly fear what they will say."

He picked up a slim white slab and placed it on his lap.

"This is your long-range communications device?"

"Yes." He ran his fingers along the narrow edges.

"None of your equipment has a viewer."

"Correct."

"Do you want me to leave?"

"There is no need." He sat very still, his hands on either side of the slab.

"Are you using an EM carrier wave? Herman's people may have the house under surveillance."

"They will not detect my transmission."

Aisha, identifying sharply with her Stone Age ancestors, fell silent.

Then Titek began to speak.

She had assumed that listening to the Negami communicating would be like listening to someone speaking a language of which she had no knowledge: say, Korean, Swahili, or Eskimo. Titek had a larynx and tongue almost identical to her own, and the instrument dictates the sound. But what she heard was something totally unexpected.

He opened his mouth—she could see that much with her sensystem—as if he were going to speak. But then the words seemed to literally die on his lips. All that came out was a throaty sigh. Sometimes, he seemed to hum tunelessly, as if to himself—but not to himself. Sometimes he made sounds reminiscent of distress, or sadness. Once, although no sound came from the slab, he stopped abruptly, as if he had been interrupted.

After five minutes he fell silent and removed his hands from the device. He sat with his head bowed.

"What's happening?" asked Aisha.

"They are conferring."

"Who?"

"The leaders of my mission."

"You told them everything? So quickly?"

"Yes." There was a tremble in his sigh. "We can do nothing now until they decide what is best."

She lifted her chin and thrust out her lower lip. "But you already know what they will decide."

"You hear that in my voice?"

"Yes," she whispered. "It is full of unspoken good-byes."

"Once again, you are perfectly...." He sniffed, and wiped at his eyes. "Correct. I fear this is the end of my Greek adventure."

"It's not fair," cried Aisha. "I want to take you to Palmyra, to the Tombs of the Nobles in Luxor, to Petra, to the Citadel of Kirkuk! I want to bring alive all the stories of the ancient world for you. I want you to see all these things, so that I can see them, too. I cannot bear to lose this."

Titek lowered his chin to his breast, and looked up at her with a sadness she could not see. "I am so sorry. I want these things, too."

"Maybe.... Does it have to be forever? Maybe some day...?"

"Dr. Thanau—may I have the honor to call you by your given name?"

"I think that is well past time."

"Yes...it is past time. Aisha, there will be no 'some day.' If I am any judge of the future, my people and I will leave your beautiful Earth. Within two days, we will be a memory—and we will not come back."

"No...!" Aisha slumped forward. "No."

"I am so sorry."

"Because of what I did!"

He raised himself onto his knees and reached out to her. "Oh, my dear Aisha, have I led you to believe that? No, no!" He walked on his knees to the bedside and took her hands. "You must dismiss this errant thought! Please. It would make me so unhappy to leave you thinking that! I would slit my throat—literally! What has happened today is only the final nail in a coffin so full of nails it is a veritable pincushion! There is a long line of such incidents leading directly to this moment. We have had a sneaker's suspicion for years that it was a mistake to come here. We can no longer avoid the truth: your planet is...too young."

"What do you mean?"

He sat back on his heels, resting the hands that clasped hers on her knees. "I have told you—we do not visit primitive planets. Earth barely met our criteria, for although you received the first signals from other planets almost a century ago, you had never had any real-time communication with alien species. But we were so keen to sneak a peek into the past—and as I have said, the history of your planet is so remarkably preserved. We bent over backwards to convince ourselves it would be all right to come! And so we came...but from the very first it was impossible to avoid noticing the signs of disaster."

"Such as?"

Titek cleared his throat. "For one thing, we were shocked at the ease with which the American government permitted us to set up our mission. Such trust in the absence of supporting evidence to warrant it is a symptom of a very primitive culture indeed. But since we knew there were wiser heads of state in Europe and Africa—none of whom was so foolish as to invite us to build an embassy within a stone's throw of their dooryard—we told ourselves it would be all right. Many similar excuses have been made. But all the time, two forces have warred against one another in our mission: the desire to stay, and the need to go. We bided our time until we could get out in the field, telling ourselves that would be the real test."

"I guess you got that right."

"Yes." He looked up at her with a sad smile. "It did not take long to find out the truth. I knew the jiggle was up that first day, when I discovered your blindness. I reported our conversation to my mission, as I was duty bound to do, knowing well full that the revelation meant the beginning of the end. Our guidelines had already been bent so far by the foolishness we had endured over the years from the Commission, I knew one more such revelation would rend them asunder."

He tightened his fingers around her hand. "This is why I worked so hard, Aisha, and showed so little interest in social frivolities—I knew I would not have much time. And then today...."

"Today you discovered that I had colluded with Mr. Herman to spy on you."

"Well, not exactly…. We never trusted Mr. Herman, and the details of his possible subterfuges mean nothing. No. The last straw that broke the camel's back was that in his primitive ignorance of the basic tenants of civilized behavior, this palooka was so unsophisticated as to take something that could be missed, and, more to the point, was incapable of adequately covering his tracks by leaving us any alternative explanation! He has stepped into the spotlight despite our best efforts to turn a blind eye to what was going on. If this were to continue, it might seriously harm Earth's continuing development! We must go—for your sakes. For whatever benefit we might derive here will be tiny indeed compared to the damage we might do. We do not wish to desecrate the temple, dear Aisha."

Aisha cleared her throat. "Let me make sure I've got this straight." She pulled the card he had given her out of her pocket. "The fact that Herman has been spying on you doesn't upset you."

"No."

"But the fact that you have cold hard evidence that he did so, does."

"Exactly."

"Aha. That makes no sense at all."

"Yes, I know. That is the point I've been trying to make for days. We are too far apart. Too far to explain why we do what we do. This is the mystery of life, is it not? The impossibility of predicting what the future holds. Would our Stone Age friend—or even a resident of Mycenea, or Ur, or Catypetal—think that it 'made sense' for you to spend a third of your life sitting at the keypads, wearing your comm loop, and working with trinary data resources?"

"No. All right. I give up." She put the card in his hand. "I accept that I don't need to know or understand everything."

Titek took the card from her. "I only wish the Zealots could be as wise!"

"I'm glad you approve. But still, I wish you had completed your work."

"My time here has been short, but—" He turned his head as if he had heard something. "Excuse me." He left her and returned to his former position on the floor.

He made very few sounds. He held the white slab in his lap for less than a minute. Then he put it back in his suitcase.

"What?" she asked.

"As I told you." His voice sounded strange.

"There is something else; something even worse."

Titek puffed out his cheeks. "The Zealots have demanded that I be censured—yes, that is close to the meaning—for allowing one of our data repositories to fall into the hands of the Earth gov—"

"There are Zealots at the mission in Virginia?"

"No—on my world."

"The mission communicated with your planet that fast?"

"Yes."

"What does that mean, censured? What will they do to you?"

"That will depend. They may pretend they are only concerned because I have been the means of contaminating your species. But they will also try to nail me for having the gall to enlighten an inferior species with our superior knowledge."

Aisha's mouth opened. "But you didn't give Herman the card on purpose!"

"No. And I will vigorously defend myself by making that point. They may, however, try to isolate me from the society of my fellows so that I do not get the chance to make my case. Be that as it may, it is not for myself that I am concerned, dear Aisha. Not for myself. This turnip of events is...most distressing—for both our worlds."

Aisha felt her chest tighten. "Please explain."

"I have had a distressing forethought. I believe the Zealots will try to withhold my work from the general public." Titek raised his knees and hugged them to his chest. "I have told you the Zealots are headed down what many of us fear is the path to doom and destruction. What I have not told you is that their certainty of their own infallibility is leading them to the belief that they—as the model society—are the rightful rulers of the galaxy. Under the guise of wanting to 'help,' they have begun to talk about taking over leadership roles on other planets—and changing our interstellar mission guidelines to do it."

She shook her head in disbelief. "How could they possibly think they have the right to do that?"

"They do not believe that other sentient societies will evolve naturally along the same path as we have. They believe it is their destiny to 'teach' others our way. They do not talk in terms of 'advanced' and 'primitive,' which are two points along the same continuum, separated only by time. They speak only of 'superior' and 'inferior,' which are the opposite sides of a coin, separated by space forever. They will try to repress my work not only because it refutes their belief, but because they will never accept that we have anything to learn from an inferior society."

"Like my first husband and the books...."

"Yes. Like him, they will never look at my work unless forced to."

"The fools.... If this comes true, maybe it is best then if the Negami do leave Earth."

"We will leave. But Aisha, it is my deepest fear that, in perhaps a few hundred years, my people will return not as harmless researchers, interested in art for art's sake—but as conquerors in search of interstellar dominion."

A shiver ran down her spine. "Then we have to do something."

"It's too late. The dye has been cast."

"It's not too late! It hasn't happened yet; you're just talking about what you think might happen! We still have your work. It can be used to stop this."

"Could have been used, yes."

"Can still." Aisha clenched her fists.

"I have discussed this in depth with my mission. The loss of the data repository has given the Zealots the upper hand. I have lost credibility and there is nothing to be done."

"Of course there is."

"What?"

"Isn't it obvious? We can get the card back!"

Titek shook his head sadly. "I fear not."

"Why not?" Aisha clucked her tongue impatiently. "You've been talking to me with great eloquence about how your civilization is so damned advanced that we're like Stone Age people by comparison. You got here from I forget how many light-years away. Tell me you can't walk through a simple force field and pick a mobius lock or two!"

"There is a difference between having the ability to do something and having the right to do it."

"Please!" Aisha threw up her hands. "Herman stole something that is yours! You have a right to get it back."

"Not while I am a visitor to these shores. It would be against everything I believe in. Do you not yet fully appreciate our commitment to noninterference?"

"No. I only see an exercise in rhetoric, useless for practical purposes."

"I assure you, it is not so. I mean what I say. I cannot stoop to Mr. Herman's level by attempting to reclaim the data repository any more than I can eat pork chops."

"A vivid analogy," said Aisha quietly. "However, you forget that in my uncivilized way, I can and do eat pork chops."

"My dear Aisha—"

"Forget it." Aisha put her hands on her hips. "I may not understand your guidelines, but I don't have to understand them to apply them. I get the picture. It is so basic to your society and character for you not to interfere with Earth that you won't even defend yourself if you are attacked. Right?"

"Right."

She pointed a forefinger at him. "And I'm betting that means you can't try to stop me if I decide to do the defending, can you."

"Oh, my." Titek put his hands to his cheeks.

"Can you?"

Titek shook his head.

Aisha set her jaw behind a thin smile. "Herman has been staying in one of the old mansions on the other side of the marina. As I see it, I have two choices—I can confront him, or I can do a little breaking and entering."

"Oh, no!" Titek scrambled up and sat beside her. "You must not do that! It is illegal!"

"It may be illegal but it's not immoral. I'm a native of these shores and it is my duty to protect my guest! A duty I regained when I told you the truth. Don't bother to try to stop me. "

"All right." He took her hand in his. "I will not try to stop you, Aisha. But I will try to…guide you toward the path with the maximum possibility of success."

"You will?" She cocked her head. "Wouldn't that be against your guidelines?"

"I...do not know. I did not expect this. We have entered a gray zone where my knowledge of the right ways does not govern. I fear that like Margaret Mead, my native attitudes have been skewered. I only know that, if you are determined to do this, I must help you as much as is humanely possible." He raised her hand and shook it. "Listen to me. You must not risk attracting the long arm of the law by an illegal entry. Neither must you confront Mr. Herman."

"Those are my only two options."

"There is a third alternative." Titek glanced cautiously around the room, as if making sure no one was listening. "You have a great advantage over Mr. Herman, which you must not give up by an untoward display of animal aggression. To whit: he has no idea that you are now working against him. You must use this advantage to ambush him and, using your superior wits and verbal nimbleness, discover the location of the data repository!"

Aisha raised a corner of her mouth. "That is a fine idea. But...I have never excelled at the art of persuasion. Nor am I a mind reader. And don't forget, I will have trouble seeing something that small in a house I am unfamiliar with." She gestured toward the box of cards on the floor.

"Perhaps. Perhaps...not!" He raised her hand to his lips. "Consider this: in my studies I have found a similarity across all languages regarding the verb 'to see.' It has its primary meaning: to see with the eyes. But there is always a metaphorical meaning: to understand. I cannot help you to see—I do not have the medical skills for that, even if it were permissible for me to use them. But I will...loan you something...that may help you to see—metaphorically speaking."

"You've lost me again."

"As I told you, my people have a tool for communication, a highly advanced technology that most assuredly owes its origin to the day my long-dead and highly revered ancestors first scratched a pictograph in a rock although we have no historical record of that highly significant event. I shall let you borrow this tool...for a little while."

"Wait just a minute." She gripped his hand. "This sounds like a fancy way of saying you're going to give me your technology. Isn't that just as bad as losing the card to Herman?"

"Not at all!" He shrugged, patting her hand. "It is a nothing. To use our favorite analogy, it is like lending your comm loop to your Stone Age friend for a moment so that she may talk with her sick child far away, and then taking it back. What secrets are revealed? What technical knowledge? What clues as to the myriad other uses to which the loop may be put?"

"And what if I keep it?"

"I know you will not." He detached his hand from hers.

"You can't pretend to be sure of that—not when you yourself know how often I have justified my actions if I thought it might help me see."

"I mean, I *know* you will not keep it…." Raising his hands to his ear, he removed the small stud with its green gem, and held it up.

"What?" She pinched her fingers together and looked at the earring.

He said nothing. Brushing at her hair, he removed the circle of gold she wore in her ear, and replaced it with the jewel.

"What's this? An external transceiver?" She moved her fingers to focus in on her ear. Just a jewel, like a green diamond, set in gold. She moved her hand to get a look at the back.

"Keep still." His fingers tugged at her earlobe.

Aisha lowered her hands. "What good will it do? Doesn't it take two people to communicate?"

He sat back. "It only takes one to understand."

She heard his voice—and the voice and the words were like the red color of the rose, or the fragrance; something that decorated the rose, but was not the rose itself. Behind and within the voice and the words—the color and the scent—was the delicate aura and shape of meaning; that which distinguished the rose from all other things that were red and smelled nice.

"What the hell is this?" she whispered.

"Do you see?"

"Yes!" She had no doubt of his meaning. *Do you understand*, he meant. "I see!"

"Now we will do a little test, to make sure I have adjusted the device properly. If I get it wrong, it will cause you a headache."

His voice was the same, but the shape beneath it was instantly distorted. The aura jangled and the colors jarred, and the thought shaped itself in her mind: *that is not true; I am in no danger of having a headache or any other side effect; he has said this to check if the device is working.*

"Oh my God." She reached out and gripped his arm. "When you said you couldn't lie, you didn't mean you were physiologically or sociologically incapable of lying, you meant you *couldn't lie*—because everyone who heard you would know you were lying."

He nodded. "On my world, lies are a social euphemism, an anachronistic metaphor designed for politeness—like your greeting conventions—or art—like your metaphor—and not for deception. I have little experience with them. How did I do?"

"Very badly. No—fine! But, with this," she touched her ear, "it was so obvious you were lying."

"Yes." He folded his arms across his breast and smiled—and she could see the smile in his words. "The device will not allow you to read minds, in the sense of browsing through someone's mind as you would a book. Without the 'peripherals,' as you would call them, you will only be able to tell whether or not a person is speaking the truth. Although, depending on how well the device interfaces with your cerebral cortex, you may be able to tell what a person is really thinking when they are speaking."

"I did that! When you said you feared I would get a headache, I knew you were lying, but I also knew you were checking to see if the device was working! The thoughts just came to me!"

"That is gratifying. You now have a secret weapon with which to defeat our adversary."

She turned her head from side to side. "But how does it work?"

"As you can imagine, the technology is complex. But the principle is not. Indeed, we have spoken of it often. At what moment, in what place, does an idea become a thought, and what determines whether or not you will package that thought into words? Who knows? I do not. But it is that magical moment when the thought is transformed into the word, just before speech, that activates the device. Or rather, it is the neurochemical change that takes place in the brain at that moment. It is not necessary for the person to actually speak the words aloud, only to intend to speak; to shape the thoughts into words in the mind as if for speech."

She nodded absently. "I understand. That is what you did when you communicated to your mission, isn't it."

"Something like it, yes. Although naturally what I do is rather more complex. You only have access to the 'lite' version."

"Does it come with directions?"

"There is no need. You must merely listen on two levels. It will not be hard. No harder than reading a work of fiction and keeping track of the dialogue, which represents what is known to both speakers, as well as any expository phrases, which represent the thoughts of one speaker, but which the other does not know."

She shook her head, unable to hide her smiles. The words were so beautiful, so true. "It's an extraordinary sensation.... The words sound like music...."

"Now it is my turn to share your delight in a new experience. I fear I take it for granted."

She touched her ear again, fingering the little jewel. "You've had this turned on the whole time you've been here?"

"Yes. And I don't mind sharing with you that it has made communicating with your species very difficult."

"Because we can't reciprocate; we can't know your true thoughts?"

"No—because you do not know your own."

The words took shape, and were like crystal—clear, hard, beautiful. "You could have turned it off."

He shook his head. "When the device is worn for long enough, there is a permanent adjustment of the cortex. When I turn it off, the more complex applications are unavailable, but this simple seeing of the words—"

"Wait a minute!" Aisha gripped his arm. "You knew! You knew everything I had done!"

"Not nearly everything. I tried to avoid the subject as much as possible. But, yes, I had a general's idea."

"Why didn't you say something? Why didn't you tell me you knew I was deceiving you?"

"Ah. But you weren't deceiving me, were you? That is the key point. What good would it have done to tell you what I knew? I could not undo your arrangement with Mr. Herman, even if I was so gauche as to confront you. Furthermore, such a revelation would have surely ended my visit, one way or the other—just as it has done, now. And I so wanted to carry on with my research."

"You just watched it happen...without trying to stop it...?"

"How could I? I did not know for certain how it would work out. Have I not explained many times? We do not live like you; our preoccupations are different from yours. This is not our way! It is not my place to say that you should do this or that, or to try and force someone else to make a choice just because it is good for me."

The humility behind his words, and the humanity, unfolded in her mind with an intricate symmetry that took her breath away. She held out her hands to him, and he took her in his arms and held her tight.

After a while, he pulled a wisp of her hair from across his mouth, and spoke. "Are you sound of mind and body?"

She grinned into his collar. "Yes."

"Good. For we must lay our plans swiftly. We have little precious time left in which to prepare for you to turn the proverbial tablets on Mr. R.H. Herman!"

Ω   Ω   Ω

R.H. Herman eased his pink feet into the soup tureen and sucked in air between his teeth. His wife had been right: he should have worn the wingtips. He had always been proud of his appearance, but with his thirty-seventh birthday nearing, he wondered if it wasn't time to pay more attention to comfort than style. But really—who would have thought that feet could hurt like this? Damned crooked stairways. Damned mountainous island. Damned inconvenient country! No wonder Greece had never made a mark on the international scene.... He eased his head back, keeping his eyes on the oversized video screen on the opposite wall, and reached for the glass of whiskey at his elbow.

The doorbell rang. "Hades..." He looked around. Damned old house! It was supposed to be fitted with all the modern accoutrements, and it did lock up tight as a drum, but.... He spotted a vox patch on the wall nearby. "System," he said. "Door comm. Yes?"

Damned thing'd better work…. "YES?"

"It's Aisha Thanau, Mr. Herman."

He rolled his eyes and raised his upper lip in distaste. "Dr. Thanau! This is a pleasant surprise." Like toothache, or an ex-girlfriend dropping by the house. "I hope everything is all right?"

"Unfortunately not, Mr. Herman. But I don't want to stand here at your door and tell the neighborhood about it."

"I'll be right there." He looked down at his feet. He had forgotten the towel. Oh, never mind. Damned old blind woman wouldn't be able to see how much water he spilled.

Ω   Ω   Ω

He raised his brows as he ushered her in. There was a stain on the front of her galabeya, and her straggly gray hair hung limp around her face. "Don't you look nice," he said jovially. "Forgive my bathrobe, Doctor. I was just running a tub when you rang."

Aisha's sightless eyes wavered down to his wet feet. "As you know I can't see much detail with my sensystem. You could be naked as a jaybird for all the difference it would make to me." She stalked past him into the salon.

"But that wouldn't be very professional of me, would it?" And wouldn't she just love it, the old nympho…. "What did you want to discuss?"

She stood in the center of the salon and stuck her chin out. "You've got a problem. Titek left the island an hour ago on a chartered boat. He knows you went through his things while we were out today. Nice job."

Cold panic rose in Herman's chest. "I see. Well, you're right. That doesn't sound good. But let's not leap to conclusions." Keep it cool, Bobby-boy, until you find out how much she knows…. "Please sit down and tell me what happened."

Aisha lowered herself into a chair. "We got back from Delos about seventeen hundred. It was a productive day, and he seemed pleased with his work. Happy. But the minute he opened the drawer where he kept his processor, he knew something was wrong. He told me someone had gained access to his processor and had probably uploaded everything."

"Impossible. My people left no trace. We didn't alter anything." How could they, when the fools hadn't even been able to make the damned thing work.... "He's guessing."

"There was a bit of paper under a corner of the processor. It had been moved."

He laughed. "You're kidding me, right?"

"I never kid, Mr. Herman. Didn't you watch old spy movies in your youth?"

"Of course not." What the hell was she talking about?

"It's a simple tale." She put her bag on the floor beside her and crossed her legs. "Titek called the Negami mission to ask for instructions. They told him to pack it in; break camp; pull up stumps. And get this—the reason was that although the Negami don't mind being spied on a little, they just couldn't stand finding out about it. Seems we are too incompetent for them to rationalize their continued presence. They're worried we're so pathetically unable to protect ourselves that they might accidentally do irrevocable damage to our low-to-medial culture. Oh well! Easy come, easy went."

"What are you saying?" Damn her sarcastic way of talking.... He needed facts!

"I think I just said it. They're leaving. All of them. In two days."

"You mean that's what he *told* you." It couldn't be true! Not now; not when he had risked so much....

"Yes, that's what he told me. But don't count on him being deceitful." She leaned toward him and lowered her voice. "They say the Negami don't know how to lie, you know."

"Really." Well, that would explain why they never saw through the Commissioner's line.... "Then we'll say he was mistaken. A scrap of paper isn't much evidence. Was there anything else?" Please don't let her know about that card....

Asia breathed deeply and settled back in her chair. "Not that he told me."

Thank God. The situation was salvageable.... "Well then." He straightened the front of his bathrobe. "I can't believe the entire Negami mission will leave Earth because a scrap of paper was moved in a drawer. Not with all the time and money they've invested here. Not after waiting so long, and putting up with our delays."

Aisha crossed her legs. "Incomprehensible, isn't it? Alien."

"Definitely unlikely. I don't think this is going to be a problem." That was the line to take—and he'd repeat it until it came true.... "Titek has no real evidence we were there. We can easily come up with an alternative explanation for that bit of paper."

"We can?"

"The wind blew it away."

Aisha snorted. "In a locked drawer?"

"Perhaps not.... What if we simply say he was mistaken?"

"Mr. Herman. Please!"

"I'm just tossing out ideas, here!" If she was going to be that way about it..... "What if you tell them it was only you, checking inside the drawer—just before you left the house this morning. You have a spare key to that drawer, right?"

"Wrong."

"Yes you do. We'll make you one."

Aisha's fingers moved restlessly in her lap. "And what was my motivation for this bizarre intrusion?"

"Something innocent—you were looking for a misplaced data crystal."

"Too vague. How do you compensate for your inability to be specific, Mr. Herman?"

"All right, all right...." Damn her! Using words like knives.... He wouldn't mind a bit if she took the fall for this.... "What if you tell them part of the truth." That always worked well for him. "Say you were snooping, looking for something, maybe a souvenir; something from the Negami home planet."

"There was nothing in that drawer—other than his data processor—that wasn't made in Calcutta."

"Did you know that at the time?"

"No.... But, Mr. Herman." She stirred. "If I admitted to snooping for so ludicrous a reason, I would be a laughingstock in the eyes of my peers, not to mention disgraced in my community. Why should I lie for you?"

"It's not lying. It's damage control. And you do it for the same reasons you agreed to my plan in the first place." Was the hint subtle enough? He'd get explicit this time if he had to....

Her voice hardened. "I agreed to your plan for the chance to learn about alien writing systems. That chance is gone. There's nothing left for me to get out of this."

"Are you sure?" Time to get a little more direct…. "I thought it was to your potential long-term benefit if the Negami stayed."

"Why? Do you think any Negami would ever trust me again?"

"I mean, to your benefit in terms of the technological advances that might be possible." Still too vague…time to zero in…. "Communications, biomedical…." It was like dangling a baited hook in front of a blind fish….

"I see." Her eyes narrowed, and a cynical smile twisted her face. "And what reason do you have to think you will ever discover any important 'biomedical advances' from the Negami?"

"We've already made progress." Good thing, too; with that card, he'd have something to bargain with if things went sour…. "I think I can say, we have solid results."

Aisha's words dripped with scorn. "Really, Mr. Herman. I find your attempts to further drag me into your web of intrigue by baiting me with these stale bits of empty promise disgusting."

Herman's spine stiffened. "I'm afraid the shock of what happened today has led you to form a false impression of my motives, Doctor." Vicious hag….

"On the contrary, Mr. Herman, it has made me see who you truly are." She pointed a finger at him. "Which is nothing more than a greedy and manipulative gangster; a man with no talents other than a quicksilver tongue, who has attained his status by telling people what they want to hear. You are a liar. The truth is you have found out nothing from the Negami, and I know it."

"I can't help what you think, Doctor." Her calling him a liar— she must be getting senile. "I can only assure you, we know more than we are at liberty to say."

"I bet. The only question is, who is 'we?'"

"I am sorry you question my loyalty. Fortunately, other, more clear-sighted people, do not." Fortunate indeed—he had to find a way to keep the Negami on the planet or the Secretary would kill him!

"If the Negami leave, it will be your fault," she sneered. "Your reputation will be ruined, Mr. Herman, and you won't have a thing to show for your pains."

"I think I'd be able to land on my feet." Especially with that card tucked away in his shaving kit as insurance....

She was silent, her eyes staring unseeing at the floor.

"Doctor Thanau?" Was she ill? Or merely out of ammunition....

She raised her chin. "Yes."

"Doctor, can't we please stop this speculation and get back to the problem at hand? Can't we somehow find a way out of the present situation in a way that will satisfy us both?"

"I doubt it." She took a deep breath. "But I thank you, anyway, Mr. Herman."

Herman stared at her in surprise. "For what?" What was she so smug about all of a sudden....

She smiled, and put her hand in her pocket. "For thinking of my best interests."

Herman jumped. "Hey!" The lights went out, leaving the room in total blackness.

"What?" asked Aisha.

"The lights are out. Damn this place!" Maybe when his eyes became more accustomed....

"Probably a central computer glitch. It happens. They'll be back on soon."

Not even a crack of light through the screens. "Why is there no emergency lighting?" He'd wanted security, but not for the place to be hermetically sealed!

"These mansions are government renovations. They have preserved the old-fashioned flavor of the architecture as much as possible. Take these lovely archways, for example...."

"I can't see a thing!"

"No, really? What a shame."

He gripped the arms of his chair. He had always hated the dark.... "System! Windows, unscreen! Damn...." What an idiot he was—sending a vox command when the power was out....

"Relax, Mr. Herman. Where are the candles?"

"Candles? I don't have any candles!"

"They have their uses—for decoration, birthdays, or to create an

92

atmosphere of light romance."

"I never bought a damned candle in my life!" Stairs! Candles! What was this, the Dark Ages?

"What? Haven't you ever had a candlelight dinner with your wife? Poor woman.... But let's not fret about your personal life. Whoever equipped the house will have provided them. Blackouts on the island are not uncommon, and of course the tourists get their little thrill out of experiencing a taste of primitive life. It helps maintain the traditional feel Kimolos is famous for."

"Maybe so, but I haven't seen any, and I have no idea where they would be."

"Most probably in a cupboard in the kitchen. Which is where?"

"Left down the hall, first door on the right."

"I'll take a look."

He heard her galabeya rustle, and the scuff of her shoes on the carpet. "Watch out!" he called. "There's a big bowl of water on the floor in the hall!"

Her voice floated across the room. "Really, Mr. Herman. You'd think I was blind, the way you talk to me."

He sneered at her—quite uselessly. Bitch. She was twisted, she really was. Well, that was what made her useful—she was too arrogant to ever think she could be wrong.

He waited a couple of minutes—at least it seemed that long. Damned dark. Made you feel helpless.... Rising unsteadily, he shuffled over to the wall. His feet were still killing him... Though his hands were outstretched, he nonetheless whacked his knee against the corner of an end table. Damned....

The sounds of a cupboard being opened and rummaged through came from the back of the house. Candles! Why wasn't there emergency lighting? He found a window, and ran his hands around the frame, looking for a manual release for the shade. Not where it should have been. Damn these Europeans—still resisting the American system, which was, as always, bigger, better, and cheaper. Ah! There was the mechanism. Naturally (since the house was rated at level nine security) it was locked.

Wait a minute. He had a little flashlight in his briefcase—his wife had insisted on his bringing it, for emergencies. Where had he left it?

In the bedroom.

Keeping his knees bent and his hands low and in front of him, Herman walked unsteadily out of the sitting room and turned right. Keeping one hand on the wall, and waving the other in the air in front of him, he hobbled down the hall, his bare feet moving noiselessly on the carpet.

He remembered the bowl of water just as his big toe touched it. Oops. That was close. He stooped lower, touching the fluted edges of the tureen with his fingers as he maneuvered his way around it. Then he stood up and leaned against the wall again.

But instead of the wall, his hand made contact with the door to the cellar, which gave way at his touch. He shouted and flailed his arms as he felt himself falling, helplessly falling into a pitch darkness....

"Careful!"

A strong hand grabbed his wrist and pulled. He fell against the door jam, and sat down hard. "Oh my God!" His heart was pounding. But he was all right. He hadn't fallen. He was all right....

Her cool, low voice floated out of the darkness. "I know the situation is bad, but killing yourself won't help, Mr. Herman."

He heard the scrape of a match, and saw Aisha's bony face, deep in shadow, above him. He watched as she lit the candle, holding her forefinger alongside the match as she touched it to the wick.

"I wasn't.... I was...I went to find a flashlight." He scrambled to his feet.

"No need. There are plenty of candles, as I told you there would be. You'd better take this before I drip wax all over the rug. It's a flokati."

He took the candle from her, and limped back to the sitting room.

He found his whiskey glass, drained it, and stuck the candle in it. "Maybe I should call Central."

"There's no point. The power will come back on soon." She re-settled herself in her chair. "But if you feel you must make a fuss...."

He sat down. "No, no. Of course not."

"Now," said Aisha. "Where were we?"

"I...." It was unnerving—sitting there in the candlelight, surrounded by looming shadows. His near-fall had shaken him, too.

What the *hell* was he going to do? If the Secretary found out he had been working with the Commissioner behind her back.... "We were trying to find a satisfactory way out of the present situation...." He winced. She was right: he fell back on empty generality when he had no real knowledge.

"Yes. Upon reflection, I think I've said all I care to say on that subject, possibly with more vim than was strictly necessary. But in the end it's the same. I'm afraid I'm not going to be able to help you. Somehow I don't fancy taking the blame for your bungle."

"Please don't be hasty." He ran a hand through his hair and smiled reassuringly. Damn! Trying to use his looks to impress a blind woman—in the dark! "That was just one line of thought. If we put our heads together, we can come up with another one. A better one. You are one of the smartest people I've ever met...." He winced again. Under the circumstances, and with her sitting there looking like an alien herself, it was getting harder and harder to massage her ego with any subtlety....

"I'm sorry, Bobbie. The truth is I've developed a distaste for the whole plan. I was enjoying my work with Titek, and I deeply regret that our time together has come to an end. My own fault. I never should have agreed to your plan in the first place."

"If you hadn't, you would not have had the opportunity to meet him at all."

"One of life's paradoxes, to be sure."

"Ah!" Relief swept through his body.

"What?"

"The lights are on."

"Indeed. Then I can leave you safe in the knowledge that next time you'll know where the candles are." She put her bag over her shoulder and stood.

He tried to persuade. He tried to flatter. He even tried to bait again. He tried to call upon her sense of civic duty. But she would not talk to him, or even pay much attention to him, and left without bothering to apologize or say good-bye. Crazy old witch. He pulled out his phone and stared at it. What was he going to say? It wasn't his fault, but everyone always blamed the messenger. Maybe it would have been better if he had fallen and broken his neck. But what would his wife have said then?

Ω   Ω   Ω

Aisha lost herself in the winding alleys of the tourist market, dodging the dancing crowds and the racks of souvenirs that jutted out from every doorway. The music seemed unusually loud. Perhaps, she thought, it was the effect of the earring.

When she reached the marina she slowed to a stroll, trying to look like any other middle-aged lady out for a bit of moonlight and sea breeze. Eventually, her heart stopped beating like a jackhammer. She headed toward the north end of the boardwalk, away from the crowds.

When her sensystem told her there was no one near, she stopped and put her hand in her pocket.

It was there, the slender card—funny how all the Negami apparatuses she had seen were so two dimensional—made out of something like stiff plastic, but cool to the touch. She ran her fingers along the short edge.

Then she felt it, as she had felt it when she had taken it from Herman's shaving kit. Words starting to form in her mind. No—not words, ideas. Thoughts that came from nowhere, and reeled past like a slow-motion movie. She knew, without thinking, what the card contained, as if she had somehow accessed an index: maps, flying ships, music—what was this data repository, an encyclopedia?—geology, history, medicine.... Her hand tensed, and, as if in response to her mental hesitation, the images changed, grew more specific. Circulatory system, musculature, nervous system....

Aisha drew her hand out of her pocket. She laced her fingers together over her heart, and turned her face to the sea.

"Hey lady!" sang a soprano voice.

She turned, raising a hand. It was one of the street boys, dressed colorfully in white shirt and red sash, dancing toward her.

"Yes?"

"I'm looking for—"

She saw the shape of his words, and Titek's face in them, and how Titek had told him to look for a tall, thin woman and bring her.... She didn't hear it or see it, she just knew it in an instant.

"You found her," she said, without waiting for him to finish. "Lead the way."

The boy saluted, then shot off ahead of her down the boardwalk, glancing over his shoulder every other step to see if she was keeping up.

He led her to a small launch, moored to one of the public piers. Taking her by the hand, he helped her over the mooring ropes and onto the deck with unexpected gentleness. The launch rolled a little, interfering with the impulses she received from the sensystem. She felt herself losing her balance, and clung to the boy for a moment.

Then Titek was there, guiding her to a bench near the cabin. "Sit here while I remunerate the young man for his labors."

She nodded and leaned back, holding her bag tight to her breast.

"I am happy to see that you are unscathed by your clandestine adventure," came Titek's voice. He slid onto the bench beside her. "I was a nerve bundle during the time we were apart. Did Mr. Herman prove vulnerable to superior planning?"

"He never suspected a thing."

"Were you able to sabotage the power relay without difficulty, as you hoped?"

"Certainly. As I told you, it is possible to override the electrical system using an infrared signal. If you know the command codes. Once I spotted the optic node on the wall, it was easy."

"For someone with your combination of skills and tools, perhaps—I don't think I could have done it."

"It helps to be able to search a room without moving your eyes. And the candle gimmick worked like a charm. It gave me an excellent excuse to leave him once I knew where to go, and the candles added a suitably spooky atmosphere. Herman will never know what hit him." She reached into her pocket and pulled out the card. "This is it, I think."

Titek took it from her hand. "Yes. Thank you, Aisha. With a little luck, we may now be able to keep the damage to the bare minimum."

"Maybe they will let you continue your work, someday...somewhere...."

"Let us hope so."

But she saw the shape of his doubt, and knew that he did not hope much.

"Let us do more than hope." She set the bag on her knees and opened it. "I have something for you—souvenirs of your visit to Earth." She pulled out something wrapped in canvas and handed it to him. "This is an inscription from the tomb of Hep-fer from the Fifteenth Century BCE on limestone. I took it from a site in Abydos in Upper Egypt many years ago. I didn't think of it as stealing; I thought I deserved to have it, because it spoke to me so powerfully. But when I was up for that job with the US government, they asked me if I had ever stolen anything in a professional capacity. When I said 'no,' their lie detector blew a fuse. Well, now I give it to you. Because...." She dug into her bag again. "Here's the same inscription on papyrus from the Fourth Century BCE." She handed him a plastic tube, about twenty centimeters long. "And here it is again in a paper book, translation by Budge into English in the Nineteenth Century. And here—on CD from the Twentieth Century, and here again in the quote on the title page from my first book, published in the late Twenty-First Century, on crystal."

"Aisha...."

She recited in a low voice: "'I have carried away the darkness by my strength, I have filled the Eye of Ra when it was helpless, I am Hem-Nu, the lightener of the darkness.' I hope it will help you, and your people."

Titek touched the box, and the book, and then looked up at her. "Thank you. I am sure these treasures will make a difference on my planet. But...more than that, I am so glad to have them, for when I see them, and touch them, I will think of you, because I love you, Aisha, and will miss you more than words can say."

The shape of his thought was beautiful. It expanded to fill her mind and resonated with her entire being. She sat bathed in the joy of it.

"You'd better take this," she said, touching her ear. "Before I change my mind."

She felt his fingers on her earlobe. A slight tug, and the earring was gone. She bowed her head.

He breathed, and opened his mouth to speak, but she covered his lips with her hand, and shook her head. Then she removed her hand, and kissed him good-bye.

He led her to the edge of the launch, and helped her back up onto the pier. She touched him one last time, and then let go.

The waves lapped against the moorings as the boatman loosed the ropes. Footsteps shuffled across the deck of the launch, and there was a clatter as the cabin door closed. The sound of the engine came, loud and harsh, breaking the quiet. Then the roar diminished as the launch pulled slowly away, and, once past the safety buoys, sped into the night. Standing with her hands at her sides, she listened until she could no longer hear the purr of the motor, or the slap of the wake against the pilings. Then she pushed her hair away from her face—conscious of the bareness of her left ear—and turned away.

Ω   Ω   Ω

The urchin was swinging from the arm of an old-fashioned lamp-post some dozen meters up the boardwalk. Aisha frowned; she was in no mood for company.

He dropped down lightly and skipped up to her. "Walk you back up the mountain, Ma'am?"

She pursed her lips disdainfully. He sounded considerate, but she could tell he also wanted the fee. "How do you know where I live?"

"I took the little gentleman to your cottage last week. He said I was highly competent for one of such tender years and asked for my number in case he required my talents."

"Did he. And what did you think of him?"

"Very polite—not like most tourists. He was fun to talk to. All about potsherds and dead sea scrolls."

Aisha tilted her head to one side. "Didn't that bore you?"

"Me? Nah. I like that stuff. I'm gonna be an archeologist when I grow up."

"Then why aren't you in school getting educated?"

He looked at her blankly. "It's August, Ma'am."

"So it is. Well.... How much?" Her tone dared him to trifle with her.

"Eight," he said, but beneath his words lay a faint gray shadow, and the shadow had a different shape, and she knew—somehow—

99

that he expected her to counter-offer with seven, but that, since he lived only two stairs from her, he would do it for five.

She whirled around and raised her hands to the sea. There was nothing there. The wind whipped her hair from her face. How was it possible? The earring was gone. *If you wear the device long enough there is a permanent adjustment of the cortex.* She shivered.

"Are you all right, Ma'am?"

She turned back to him. "Five," she said. "And no argument."

"Tch," he said, and his shoulders sagged.

"But…. If you're really serious about wanting to be an archeologist, I'll hire you for the full day on Saturday, and we'll hop down to Alexandria and visit the new French dig. Travel expenses and lunch included. And if you mind your keys and pews and prove that you can take good care of an old blind lady…we might make it a regular arrangement. I've just realized I need to do quite a bit of field work for the new book."

"Yes, Ma'am!" His shoulders straightened, and he took her arm eagerly. "Alexandria! Wow…. I've never been to Egypt…."

She smiled indulgently at his excitement, and lowered her hands to let him lead her through the night.

Author's Apology

Prometheus has been a favorite subject with the poets
(Thomas Bullfinch, c. 1860)

There is no way of knowing how or when the Prometheus Legend was created, or how many generations heard it told and passed it on before the invention of the alphabet allowed the contemporary version to be written down. The first sketchy references appear in the work of the Greek poet Hesiod (8th c. BCE). Prometheus, we learn, was one of the Titans—gods who were the first inhabitants of Earth and later engaged in a war with another group of gods, the Olympians. Prometheus, whose name means "forethought," escaped an unpleasant fate by switching sides and helping Zeus win. But he was constantly at odds with the Olympians. He defied Zeus repeatedly—by creating human beings, giving them fire and showing them how to cheat the gods, and by refusing to use his foresight to reveal a plot against Zeus. For his disobedience, Zeus caused him to be "bound with inextricable bonds, cruel chains, and drove a shaft through his middle, and set on him a long-winged eagle, which used to eat his immortal liver" (Hesiod, *Theogeny*).

If stories were solely the narration of unique adventures involving distinctive characters, one might assume that once the legend was written down, there would be nothing more to say about Prometheus. But, of course, they are not. Embedded within stories (particularly those we call myths) are multifaceted themes, the sorts of things called archetypes or motifs, which are elemental to human experience. Such themes resist definitive interpretation but remain irresistible to artists eager to have a go at interpreting. Retellings are inevitable and natural. But what explains the parade of poets, playwrights, novelists, composers and artists who, over the past 3,000 years or so, have chosen to versify, novelize, compose, paint, sculpt and otherwise revisit Prometheus? *Books in Print* lists over 2,000 books with the word Prometheus in their title. Compare that with Poseidon (29), Hera (35), Zeus (50), Oedipus (272), and Pandora (389). That's a lot of interpretation for a story that can be summarized in half a paragraph!

The Themes

The Prometheus Legend has the advantage over other myths in that it has three distinguishable themes: 1) creation; 2) fire-theft, and 3) torment. Each theme has its attendant images and story elements, particularly the last two. The theft and subsequent gift of fire symbolize the enlightenment of humanity. The torment of rock and eagle represents the price that is paid for that enlightenment.

Torment. Greek vase, c. 550 BCE.

The many treatments of the Legend are distinguished one from another in two ways: 1) by the era in which the writer or artist lived, and 2) by the theme on which he or she focused. They are alike in that they each add, subtract, and change details and characters, and (in the written forms) make no bones about presenting

Creation. Origin unknown.

alternative endings. It comes as no surprise that each treatment contradicts all the others at every turn. Was it an eagle or a vulture? Did it eat his heart or his liver? Was his wife's name Asia or Clemense? Or was that his mother? Did Zeus punish him for stealing fire, or for not revealing that plot? Was he up there for ten thousand or thirty thousand years? Was he ever freed? Was it Herakles or Hermes who freed him? Did Prometheus give humanity fire, science, astronomy, or the alphabet? Surrounded by such chaos, the legend as Hesiod jotted it down must surely be all but unrecognizable.

But it is not. The universality of its themes, combined with the specificity of the images that convey those themes, give a myth its vitality, not the style of the writer or the choice of ending. Times change, kingdoms rise and fall, but the images of molded clay, raised torch, and eagle's claw and the themes they represent, have no expiry date. If anything, the retellings have revitalized the tale, as the repetition and inevitable amendment over the centuries must have done in pre-literate days. The only difference is that since the intervention of writing we have evidence of the disagreement and change. This is no paradox. The purpose of myth is not to explain, but to explore.

Fire-theft. Ancient Greek mosaic.

Classical Greece and Rome

The Greek playwright Aeschylus wrote his stunning *Prometheus Bound* circa 467 BCE. As evidenced by the title, Aeschylus focused on the torment theme; creation and fire-theft are there, but relegated to backstory. It is the victory of ignorance over enlightenment—of brutality over generosity—that drives the play. Prometheus rages against the world in general and Zeus in particular, while the venomous Hermes taunts him and tempts him to give in by turns. And all the while the Chorus—the voice of the masses—whispers of the wisdom of bowing down to might even when might is most definitely wrong: *Ah, they are wise / Who do obeisance, prostrate in the dust, / To the implacable, eternal Will.*

Aeschylus is responsible for fleshing out the story—or at least for writing down a lot more detail from contemporary oral versions. As far as Hesiod is concerned, Prometheus stole fire. Period. But to Aeschylus, fire is a complex metaphor for knowledge, science, language, indeed all things that separate humankind from the animals:

> *Prometheus* (speaking of humankind).
> In the beginning...
> They dwelt in burrows of their unsunned caves
> ...but utterly without knowledge .
> ...until I the rising of the stars
> Showed them, and when they set, though much obscure.
> Moreover, numbers, the most excellent
> Of all inventions, I for them devised,
> And gave them writing that retaineth all,
> The serviceable mother of the Muse.

Few students of comparative literature would disagree that the Prometheus Legend reaches the apex of its power with Aeschylus. That didn't slow down the imitators, or course. Back in the olden days, it was anticipated and accepted that a poet or artist would have a go at the classical canon. "Originality" in storytelling is a modern concept—one might almost say, "delusion" after this brief check of the record, which shows that the archetype is antithetical to originality, indeed appears to have no certain origin at all.

Thus, hot on Aeschylus' heels we find such worthies as Herodotus (c. 440 BCE) and Plato (c. 360 BCE) recording or analyzing Prometheus' exploits. Aristophanes (the Woody Allen of his day) lampoons Prometheus in his comedy, *The Birds* (414 BCE). In the early days of the Christian Era, Pausanius, Apollodorus, Ovid, and who knows who all else took their turn. And that's only the writers.

The earliest surviving artwork is a Corinthian vase, made about 550 BCE. Its presentation of the artist's chosen theme (torment) is as stark as the words of Aeschylus. This sets a precedent: as we trace the Legend down through the centuries, Promethean art and literature follow parallel paths, each medium reflecting, as noted above, the preoccupations of its times.

Renaissance

Thanks to the ensuing Dark and Middle Ages, the record is blank until the early 16th c., when Prometheus reemerges as a favorite subject of the European art world. Times have changed. The starkness and lack of sentimentality of the classical era have been replaced by the passion and excess of the Renaissance. But the themes remain the same, though for a while the painters have sole possession of them. It is only in 1773 that the literary thread reappears, when Goethe wrote "A Poetic Monologue: Prometheus." It never disappears again.

Creation. The Myth of Prometheus, *Piero di Cosimo, 1515.*

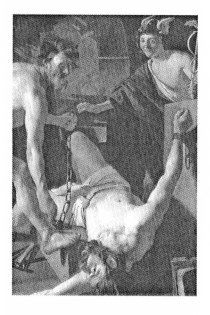

Torment. Prometheus Being Chained by Vulcan, *Dirck van Baburen, 1623. Note the delighted expression on the apple-cheeked face of Hermes as he watches. This painting, and one of similar composition by Jacob Jordaens* (Prometheus Bound, *1640*) *were inspired by the* Chained Prometheus *of Peter Paul Rubens (1611/12), which started a rage for the upside-down Prometheus.*

The 19th Century

In 1818, Percy Bysshe Shelley wrote his long poem, "Prometheus Unbound." This popular work features the first acknowledgment and explanation of the many contradictory versions of the Legend. Shelley writes in his preface:

> The Greek tragic writers, in selecting as their subject any portion of their national history or mythology, employed in their treatment of it a certain arbitrary discretion. They by no means conceived themselves bound to adhere to the common interpretation or to imitate in story as in title their rivals and predecessors. I have presumed to employ a similar license.

Selah. Shelley (torment theme again), used his license to recast Prometheus in the double mold of Romantic emotionalism and Christian martyrdom:

> The moral interest of the fable is so powerfully sustained by the sufferings and endurance of Prometheus. The only imaginary being, resembling in any degree Prometheus, is Satan; and Prometheus is, in my judgment, a more poetical character than Satan, because, in addition to courage, and majesty, and firm and patient opposition to omnipotent force, he is susceptible of being described as exempt from the taints of ambition, envy, revenge, and a desire for personal aggrandizement. (From the Preface)

Torment. Prometheus, *by Gustave Moreau, 1868. Note the vulture and the Christ-like face.*

Despite this Satanic feint, Shelley (and many a Christian commentator down the years) is besotted with the obvious parallels between Prometheus on his mountain and Christ on the cross (suffering for humanity; wound in the side, etc.). The idea of the willful classical god is gone. Prometheus is a monotheist whose first words are in homage to a higher authority (and he doesn't mean Zeus). Shelley glories in his hero's Christ-like forgiveness. Compare this on the chastening effects of suffering—*I am changed so that aught evil wish / Is dead within*—with the words of Aeschylus' pagan hero—*I hate all the Gods, / Because, having received good at my hands, / They have rewarded me with evil.* You don't catch Aeschylus' Prometheus pondering what a better man he'll be for what he's been through. His bitterness is as enduring as his strength of will to sit it out.

Torment. Prometheus Bound, *by Christian Schussele, 1870. Note the waves in the Caucasus.*

Alfred Lord Byron had written his short poem, "Prometheus," in 1816. Mary Shelley kept the creation theme alive by subtitling her 1830 *Frankenstein* "A Post-modern Prometheus." In the middle of the century, Victor Hugo wrote his poem "Entre Geants et Dieux" (Between Giants and Gods).

The Romantic composers found inspiration in the Legend, too. Ludwig von Beethoven's only ballet (1801) was called "Creatures of Prometheus." Franz Schubert wrote a song called "Prometheus" in 1818. Franz Liszt wrote a symphonic poem with the same title in 1860.

Torment. Prometheus, *by Briton Riviere, 1889.*

By the latter half of the 19th c. paintings proliferate, and references to one or another of the Promethean themes appear in countless books, stories, and poems. With the writers and artists of the Western Hemisphere adding their names to the lists, it becomes impossible to keep track.

Fire-theft. Frieze on the old AT&T Building in NYC.

The 20th Century

Alexander Scriaben composed his "Prometheus, Le Poeme du feu" (Poem of the Fire) in 1908. Samuel Barber wrote his "Incidental Music for a Scene from Shelley" in 1933. So our modern world finds Prometheus alive and well in music, word and image—and everywhere else. A rare Earth metal is named after him; a moon of Saturn; a mountain in Nevada; dozens of sites on the Internet.

Nothing has changed—or has it? Prometheus has certainly gotten a lot younger as the centuries have ticked by, perhaps a sign of the slow rise to power of our youth culture. The beard is gone, so too the big muscles. At times, the mighty Titan appears positively boyish—a trend no doubt strengthened by the famous art deco statue in Rockefeller Plaza. This trend verges on the absurd with the Maxfield Parrish calendar for Edison Electric (1934), wherein a cherubic Prometheus skips along bearing his streetlamp *cum* torch (power by Edison).

Fire-theft. Prometheus, *Paul Manship, 1934. Rockefeller Plaza, NYC.*

Furthermore, although all three themes appear from classical to modern times, they are not present in equal numbers. Creation, lacking the conflict of the other two themes, was at its most popular during the classical age (not surprisingly, since what I am here terming Ancient Greek "legend" is quite rightly termed Ancient Greek "religion" elsewhere). No doubt the advent of Christianity helped diminish popular interest in the creation theme, while

106

at the same time boosting interest in the torment theme, for the reasons mentioned. Torment dominated Promethean art and literature from the Renaissance to the 20th c., when suddenly the fire-theft theme comes into its own. In today's Information Age, the idea of taking knowledge from those who would hoard it or charge for it and giving it freely to everyone is a powerful concept.

Fire, as a symbol of enlightenment, loses nothing over the millennia; indeed it reinvents itself with every age. Today, the name "Prometheus" means little or nothing to most of us. But if we see a statue of a man holding up a torch in front of a university, we get his point, though we may not know his name. So do the times affect the theme. The theft element has disappeared, leaving the idea of knowledge not so much stolen as preserved; passed on; kept alight.

Fire-theft. Prometheus, *Maxfield Parrish, c. 1930. From the Edison Electric calendar.*

Fire-theft. In our modern world, it is perhaps inevitable that the Legend would turn up as the simplest form of graphic metaphor: the logo. Here are various commercial logos associated with the name, Prometheus. Observe, albeit with morbid curiosity, as the theme is reduced first to a hand holding a torch; the torch; and finally—Prometheus rarified—just the flame.

The Present Work

A child of my times, it was the fire-theft theme that drew me to write the present work. Creation is wholly absent; torment present only as a threat to Titek's future. Like Zeus, the Zealots seek to hoard their knowledge from lesser beings; like him, they punish those who disagree without mercy or reference to motive.

It is this fear of losing power through the spread of knowledge that intrigues me; that, and the suicidal (because it inevitably arouses the ire of Zeus) determination of Prometheus to proliferate that knowledge. Thus, I was eager to explore the events that led up to the fateful moment of no-return—the moment Prometheus decided to do what he had been forbidden to do, and hand over "fire"—in this case a new way of "writing" (that serviceable mother of the Muse)—to humanity.

What, I asked myself, if Prometheus had a specific reason for defying Zeus' will? Or…what if he was under duress? What if it was an accident, what if he never meant to give humanity "fire" at all? Or…what if it was stolen from him? What, I wondered (bouncing along in the ruts of many a SF writer) if the Titans and Olympians were advanced beings from outer space who landed on Earth thousands of years ago? What if they came back now, or a hundred years from now? What would they be like without a thousand years of elaboration (by storytellers more interested in audience reaction than in authenticity) to turn them into gods?

So I wrote it. And if I have ignored some parts of the story, invented others, and had the nerve to change the ending, I can only apologize, and remind you that, though I have dared to tread, page-like, in the footsteps of the gods of art and literature, I am only the latest to do so, and will most certainly not be the last.

Fire-theft transformed to Enlightenment. Wisdom, *Zurab Tsereteli, 1979, at SUNY Brockport.*

Printed in the United States
30827LVS00001B/187